JUL -- 2021

BROKEN
SPUR

Center Point
Large Print

Also by D. B. Newton and available from
Center Point Large Print:

The Savage Hills
Bounty on Bannister
Bullets on the Wind

BROKEN SPUR

A
JIM BANNISTER
WESTERN

D. B. NEWTON

CENTER POINT LARGE PRINT
THORNDIKE, MAINE

This Center Point Large Print edition
is published in the year 2021 by arrangement with
Golden West Literary Agency.

Originally published in the US by Popular Library.

The text of this Large Print edition is unabridged.
In other aspects, this book may vary
from the original edition.
Printed in the United States of America
on permanent paper.
Set in 16-point Times New Roman type.

ISBN: 978-1-64358-985-5 (hardcover)
ISBN: 978-1-64358-989-3 (paperback)

The Library of Congress has cataloged this record under
Library of Congress Control Number: 2021935080

Chapter I

Before dropping him into timber that narrowed his range, this high trail from over on the west side of the pass gave Jim Bannister some sweeping views of the country farther on. It looked to him that the mountain, all rugged bare granite here, gentled toward its foot until it became a long sweep of grass and timber, watered by flashing streams. Beyond the valley's deep trough the yonder, eastern wall was lower than this one but a good deal rougher. Taken altogether, what he saw looked to Bannister like good stock range, well protected against the rigors of Colorado's winter storms.

He had camped last night on saddle rations, under the far shoulder of the peaks, and tackled the pass in a chill red sunrise. Now the sun's warmth was welcome, in a deep sky where summer clouds sailed majestically. Bannister had thrown open his windbreaker and presently shucked out of it, to strap it behind the saddle of the dun horse. He was a big man, tall even for a time and place where men ran to rangy height. His hatbrim shaded a face the elements had darkened in odd contrast with sharp blue eyes and tawny yellow hair. His clothing and gear were well-worn and serviceable.

Serviceable too was the look of the belt and holster at his waist—each shell loop filled with brass, a wooden revolver handle thrust from the holster's mouth. He had learned never to go for long without that gun, or sleep without it close to hand. And as always when traveling into strange territory, he rode now with a wary caution.

So it was, as morning wore on and he worked his way down this ancient pass trail, that Bannister became aware he wasn't alone on the mountain.

He was still in rough terrain, broken by draws and timbered pockets where he noticed frequent signs of stock use; but now, just below a belt of pine and aspen, he made out what looked to be a fairly level stretch of bench land. Assuming adequate water and grass, it seemed likely that ranches from the valley would be in the practice of moving their herds up here, in season, to be placed on summer range. As though to confirm this, he shortly became aware of movement down there and at once pulled rein, a reflex action, as the flawless clarity of mountain air and light showed him the red hides of a pair of beef animals that all at once broke out of the brush.

A rider followed them, his horse running, his arm up and circling with a coiled rope at the end of it. Faint across the distance, Bannister heard the shout he lifted as he plunged after the cattle;

then brush and rocks swallowed them all, as completely as if they had never been.

Still working his way downward, he watched more carefully and saw more evidence—here, a feather of dust rising above a clump of trees and, yonder, a couple of horsemen who came together in a clearing, one chasing a steer ahead of him. The men paused for an exchange and then parted, the one to spur after his animal while the second moved on into the brush.

Bannister was left frowning. There seemed to be a good number of riders working these draws, apparently involved in digging cattle out in ones and twos and running them down toward the bench. This was a legitimate operation—except that high summer appeared an odd time for it. Summer was the season when, having your beef spotted where you wanted it, you left it alone to feed and put on tallow; digging them out and moving them down was an activity for the fall gather. He was a little curious at what seemed a mix-up in the timetable.

He forgot to wonder about that a minute later, when there was a rustling in the brush and a steer suddenly appeared directly in front of him. It was a big fellow, probably a three-year-old, wearing a Bar L brand and patchy-hided as though from toughing it out in all seasons here in the brush and rocks of the high mountainside. It had likely been missed in earlier roundups, with a native

7

instinct for avoiding the men who would have snaked it out of hiding and driven it off to market. Now, at sight of a rider, the massive head, wicked horns lowered, swung as the steer prepared to change directions and once more plunge away into cover.

Jim Bannister acted almost without thinking, neck-reining sharply to the left. The dun had had training as a cowhorse and knew what was wanted. It cut over sharply, heading the steer, shouldering in to prevent its escape. Bannister lacked a saddle rope but he whipped off his hat and batted it in the animal's face, at the same time loosing a yell. Horns flashed sunlight as the steer braked again and started to spin away; at once the dun cut back, and for all its wary stubbornness the animal had to let itself be turned and driven lunging down the trail with the rider pushing hard after.

Tree shadows flickered above them, hoofbeats knocked back echoes from granite outcroppings. Abruptly they came out of the pines and the trail dropped to a shallow flat, at whose far end, a hundred yards distant, Bannister glimpsed several head of cattle and riders working them into a gather. Quickly he reined in, letting the steer go. At the same moment he heard a shout somewhere to his right. He turned and saw a man on a sorrel cow-pony, staring at him.

"You!" the man yelled a second time. Now he

kicked with a heel and came spurring straight at Bannister, and as he did he pulled a saddle gun out from under his right knee.

Bannister tightened when he saw the smear of light on the rifle barrel, but by then it was already too late; he downed the first instinctive reaction and let the short gun stay in his own holster. Keeping both hands in plain view, he waited while the other pulled rein and dust from the sorrel's hoofs blew and settled. The muzzle of the carbine pointed squarely at his chest.

The face he saw above the rifle was that of a man about forty, wearing rough range clothing and a wide-brimmed hat that had long since sweated out its band. The face was sallow, lantern-jawed, dark with beard stubble. The black eyes held sharp suspicion and something even more dangerous. "What the hell do you think you're up to?" the rider demanded, in a harsh voice.

Meeting the look, Bannister replied, "I think I just ran a steer out of the brush. What do *you* think?"

"I think you got no business here on the Lease." It was a challenge, growing louder with every angry word. "I don't know you. I never seen you before."

Bannister nodded. "No, I can vouch for that. It's a new country to me—I just came over the peaks this morning. Understand there's a town called Dunbar in the valley. I was counting on this trail to take me down."

The rider neither confirmed nor corrected his impression. The black eyes continued to study him, still bright with hostility. Something in the set of his mouth, and the puckering of the skin about the eyes, gave warning that this man was holding himself on a tight leash. The hand that held the rifle at the trigger housing was pale at the knuckles, from the tightness of its grip; to see that, and hear the note of near hysteria in the other's voice, was enough to send a chill bead of sweat down across Bannister's ribs as he wondered just what sort he might be dealing with.

It was almost with a feeling of relief that he heard another horseman approaching, and turned quickly to look at the man coming up on the other side of him.

He was older than the first, his mustache and beard stubble almost white and his cheeks carved into weathered folds. Though he was armed, he made no move toward a weapon. His blue eyes held a steady shrewdness when he drew in and put his glance on both men, in turn.

"Anything the matter here?" he wanted to know.

"Didn't you see what happened?" the one with the rifle demanded. "Weren't you watching? He was running one of your Bar L steers. I'm trying to find out what he thought he was up to."

Bannister tried to keep his temper in check. "I

rather thought I was doing somebody a favor. I saw riders working the timber and judged them to be looking for holdouts; then this steer popped out right in front of me. It was only natural to try and turn him, before he could get back into those draws and lose himself."

The explanation drew an explosive snort from his challenger, but the older man frowned thoughtfully. He pulled off his hat, swept a rope-gnarled hand across sparse white hair that lay close against his skull. "Well, now," he said, nodding, "that strikes me as a neighborly gesture. Tobe, did you suppose the man wanted to *steal* him?"

"How the hell am I supposed to know what he wanted?" the first one retorted. "All I know is, I'll have nobody fooling around stock that belongs to *me*—for any reason! Hell, we none of us got more than we can spare."

"You'll get no argument on that," his friend admitted in a dry tone; but his look at Bannister, as he replaced the worn Stetson, indicated that he too might be having a little trouble holding onto his patience. "Happens this time it's one of my animals we're talking about; so you don't need to worry about it, Tobe—though I appreciate your concern. There's coffee ready at the fire," he added. "Why don't you go get some? Let me handle this."

The one with the rifle didn't like being dismissed. He glared at Bannister and his mouth worked on unspoken words that seemed to be trying to tumble out of him. A muscle of his cheek, at the corner of one eye, had begun to jerk. Bannister watched him in some alarm, having seen badly broken horses that reacted unpredictably to the rein and the whip.

The older man, though, had a quiet authority about him. When he repeated calmly, "Now, go on, Tobe," the other finally gave in, with an angry movement of his shoulders as he jerked his horse about and booted it away from there, sliding the carbine back into its scabbard as he went.

They watched the dust spurt and settle under the sorrel's hoofs. Bannister could feel the muscles that cramped his chest begin to loosen a little. He commented, "Your friend seems strung pretty tight."

"I know," the older man agreed solemnly. "Not his fault, I suppose. Some men can take their troubles in stride. Tobe Munkers builds a fast head of steam and sometimes, when things are going wrong, he ain't always able to handle it— it can be worse when he's had a shot or two of whiskey under his belt. . . . Well, anyway," the man went on, abruptly changing the subject, "I do thank you for lending a hand with that steer. One thing Tobe says is sure as hell true—ain't any of us that's been running cattle here on the Lease, who can afford to have one of them get

12

away; and this is the last gather we'll likely have a chance to make.

"How about it—can I offer you some coffee? I think we got a few biscuits and beans, too, that are maybe fit to eat."

Bannister saw the fire, built no larger than was needed to heat up the grub someone had brought along. Five men, with their saddled horses waiting nearby on trailing reins, were filling plates and coffee cups; a couple of others who were watching the twenty-odd head of cattle already collected, to prevent them bolting again for the freedom of the timber, would have their turns later.

Tobe Munkers was just now dismounting and accepting the food somebody handed him, and Bannister said, "Thanks, but if this is the right trail for Dunbar maybe I'll be riding along. I wouldn't want to bother your friend Munkers any more than I already have."

The older man shrugged. "Tobe Munkers is just going to have to get used to being bothered," he grunted, "without continually flying off the handle, every time he turns around. As for Dunbar, it's a good three hours from here; I wouldn't feel right, sending you on without a bait of something first. So, come along."

"All right. If you're sure."

Lifting the reins, the other said, "By the way, I'm Harry Lantry. What should I call you?"

13

Bannister had expected the question and had his lie ready. "Bonner," he answered smoothly. "Jim Bonner . . ."

Approaching the fire, he met the mildly curious glances of men who were used to seeing strangers drift up out of the vastness of a big land, and as casually vanish. Only Tobe Munkers lowered his tin coffee cup long enough to give the stranger a look of open hostility; but he held his brooding silence, offering no comment as the newcomers dismounted and Lantry casually introduced Bannister around.

There were too many names to catch; he gathered that a couple were small-scale stockmen, the others rode for them. Only one—a long-waisted, bowlegged fellow in a horsehide vest—paid Bannister any real attention. Sam Reeves by name, he favored the stranger with an intent scrutiny of pale-lashed eyes and suddenly blurted, "Seems like I might have seen you before."

On a New Mexico reward dodger? Bannister asked himself, while he hoped his face concealed any start the words gave him. Bannister had seen those notices, with their crude woodcut likeness and the details of the murder charge against him, that the Chicago syndicate people were having duplicated and distributed, broadcast, all through this state of Colorado now that they knew he seemed to be centering here. . . . But Harry Lantry laid the suggestion to rest with a decided shake of the head as he pointed out to Reeves, "Now, you know you ain't been anywhere I haven't, Sam, and he's a new one to me—tells me he came over the peaks this morning, headed for Dunbar."

To Bannister's relief Sam Reeves appeared to accept the verdict, though his eyes lingered on the stranger's face an instant longer before he shrugged and turned away, leaning to take the smoke-blackened coffee pot out of the coals.

There were no more questions asked of the stranger as he and Lantry filled their plates, but neither was there much of the good-natured banter one normally heard at a roundup campfire. Bannister sensed a glum and dispirited mood in these men. Two of them soon finished their eating and mounted, to relieve the pair watching the cattle and let them come in for grub. After a while, a hand named Bart Williams, who apparently worked for Lantry, put a question to his boss: "Looks to me like we've about got these pockets cleaned out. What do we do next—start working higher?"

Lantry swirled the steaming liquid in his cup. "I'd say no. We don't have the time, and the pickings are bound to get slimmer the farther up we go. We'll do better to swing north and see if we can lend the other boys a hand."

"No, damn it!" That outburst was from Tobe Munkers, who seemed still in a foul mood. "Long as I got a single head left on this mountain, I want it! You expect me to go off and leave my beef for that fellow Stroud?"

"All I'm saying," Lantry answered with studied patience, "is we're coming up to the deadline. Two more days and that's it. It's probably our own fault that we're cutting it so close—we waited too long, hoping clear to the last that it wouldn't really come to this. Now, we've just got to make the best use of what little time is left."

Sam Reeves shook his head, frowning and disturbed. "Like Tobe said, it's our beef; it's got our brands. Even if we don't quite manage to get the job done, I can't believe Frank Stroud, or anyone else, would refuse us the right to come back and finish it."

"You gonna get a court order, maybe?" Munkers retorted. "Didn't that tough hand of his—that Ridge Decker—didn't he tell me in so many words that, once Caverhill turns over the deed, Stroud ain't gonna stand for us fooling around here on the Lease, for any reason? His orders will be to run us off!"

Williams, a seasoned cowhand with a no-nonsense quality about him, gave Munkers a sidelong look. "You already told me Ridge was drunk when he said that," he reminded the other. "I kind of got the idea you both was. Maybe you said something first that got him riled. You ain't the soul of tact, you know."

Munkers whirled to glare down at the man where he sat on an aspen stump with tin plate balanced on his knee. "You sonofabitch!" he challenged loudly. "Let's see you get on your hind legs and repeat that!"

Williams merely gave Harry Lantry a look that said, "You see what I mean?" and then the older cowman was there to shoulder Tobe Munkers aside. "All right, all right!" he said gruffly. "One thing we can't afford is to quarrel among ourselves. Time's too short. They're having a rehearsal at the church this evening; the ceremony's Sunday. And that's the deadline."

"Unless it can be put off somehow," Sam Reeves suggested, without much conviction. "Something just might happen."

"I wouldn't know what it would be. Personally, I sure wouldn't put much faith in a court order, or in Frank Stroud's generosity—either one."

Jim Bannister had stood discreetly apart during all this, working at his plate of food and not wanting to interfere—just as pleased, too, to stay on the sidelines and not invite further speculation from Sam Reeves who had found his face so uncomfortably familiar. But now, as he finished eating and stepped to add his utensils to a pile beside the fire, he remarked in a casual tone, "It's none of my business, of course; but listening to your talk has got me confused. Is somebody having a wedding?"

"Emily Caverhill," Lantry answered, nodding. "Old man Caverhill's marrying off his niece."

"To this man Stroud?" Bannister pursued, more or less guessing from the scraps of conversation he'd pieced together. "How does it affect your group?"

The short-fused Tobe Munkers rounded on him, his initial hostility in no way abated. "Mister," he declared harshly, "for a thing that's none of your business, you're sure asking questions!"

Bannister nodded, not letting himself be baited. "Yes, I suppose you're right," he admitted calmly, and let the matter drop. "I thank you for the grub," he told them. "I guess I'll be getting along, if it's still three hours down to Dunbar. "He included them all in a half salute, and afterward turned away to his horse, feeling Tobe Munkers' smoldering stare against his back.

He was checking the cinch when Harry Lantry came over to join him; the old fellow was embarrassed, it seemed, and anxious to apologize. "You ain't to mind Tobe, Mr. Bonner. He's got a real big mouth."

"I don't figure to let things like a big mouth bother me too much." Bannister took the reins, ready to mount.

But Lantry was bothered, and he wanted to explain. "Like I said, Tobe gets worked up—as we all are these days. But, to answer your question: There's seven of us small-fry ranchers, running between us considerably less than a thousand head in a good season—and that depending on our being able to find suitable summer range. Up to this year we been able to use the grass here on this bench. It used to belong to a man named Holbrook, who tried to run stock up here year round but couldn't last the winters; so he finally quit and moved to Denver, and gave the bunch of us a deal to lease the bench for summer range on a year-to-year basis. Six months ago Holbrook died and his widow put the bench up for sale. We were trying, amongst us, to figure how to raise the asking price, when Arch Caverhill of the Broken Spur iron got in ahead of us and she sold to him instead."

Bannister said, "Was that legal? If your lease had an option-to-buy clause—"

The man made a face. "We never had a thing in writing. It was an oral agreement with Tom Holbrook—the kind that's served the needs of the cattle country for as long as *I* can remember. But it meant nothing," he added bitterly, "when Arch Caverhill decided he wanted a wedding present for Frank Stroud and Emily. He knew we depended on this grass to stay in business. Somehow we just never supposed Arch would do a thing like that to his neighbors—even if his spread is more'n twice the size of our outfits, put together."

"And Stroud? Is his outfit a big one?"

19

"It will be now!" Harry Lantry grunted. "Once he adds our summer range onto his! He'll be able to double his herds. He'll outgrow that place of his on Squaw Creek. The hell of it is," he said, pouring out his grievances, "you understand it's not just the Lease itself. Losing it means we're shut off from the mountain altogether. We aren't left with any choice now, but to take our herds across the other side of the valley and up into the Wishbones—and that's a damn poor substitute!"

Remembering his earlier look at yonder valley wall, Bannister could well believe this. It had appeared barren, rockribbed, with little timber showing and not much promise of grass—and in a cattle country of cramped valleys, between the confining walls of folded mountain ridges, a rancher's survival depended on keeping a balance between the summer and winter range available to him. He could only nod in sympathy as Lantry said, "This thing has put us back maybe ten years. At the very least, we're going to have to trim our herds. Some of us are going to end up losing everything."

Jim Bannister said thoughtfully, "And all because a man wants to give his niece a dowry . . ."

"I call it a bribe! Maybe Arch is scared that Emily might turn out to be an old maid—which don't make much sense to me, her being barely thirty and a good looking woman at that, besides

20

being the only one for him to leave Broken Spur to.

"Still, for whatever reason, Arch appears to be real keen on this match and I think Stroud knows it. Buying the Holbrook Lease for him may have been his price for going through with the marriage—in fact, we hear Arch is refusing to turn the deed over till after the ceremony on Sunday, which sounds pretty damn funny. At any rate, I sort of like to feel that Arch Caverhill is under some kind of pressure, because I've always thought of him as almost like a friend . . ."

He broke off abruptly, with an impatient slice of one rope-tough palm. "Time's wasting—I better get back to hunting strays. We put the job off too long, hoping to the last something might happen: now it's almost too late. The mountain is home to some of these critters that have been hiding out from us, three years and even longer. They don't like leaving, any more than we do pulling 'em out. No wonder they're hard to catch!"

He turned away, to rejoin the group that had finished their eating and were putting out the fire and packing up. Bannister called, "Good luck." After that he found the stirrup, mounted up and turned the dun once more into the downward trail leading toward the valley.

His expression was bleak. There was no way Harry Lantry, reciting the problems of himself and his friends, could have guessed he was passing on dismaying news that threw this stranger's own plans in jeopardy. Jim Bannister had ridden miles and faced uncertain risks in coming here. Now, after what he'd learned, the whole thing was suddenly doubtful enough that he actually considered whether it wouldn't be better sense to go back.

But this had been a last desperate hope, for a man who had seen most other hopes dissipate and vanish; he could not afford to give it up. Doggedly, he rode ahead . . .

At the fire, cinches were being tightened, bits replaced and utensils stowed away. Tobe Munkers, preparing to mount, gave Lantry a hard stare across the sorrel's saddle and said loudly, "You and that stranger had yourselves a right cozy chat, didn't you? Far as I could see, *you* was the one doing the talking. I suppose you loaded all our personal affairs on him."

Lantry scowled, as he felt the heat rise through his leathery cheeks and knew he was turning red. What Munkers said was much too near the truth—he supposed he *had* talked more than he should. Was it because he simply had to get it off his chest? Or was there, he wondered, something about Jim Bonner that suggested sympathy, and encouraged a man to confide in him?

Munkers read his silence and said gruffly, "Yeah, I bet you stood there and give him the

22

whole damn history—Holbrook, and the Lease, and Caverhill and all the rest of it. He pumped you dry."

"He did not!" Harry Lantry retorted quickly, in the stranger's defense. "He hardly said a word. It's just that, after we'd spoke so free in front of him, I thought he deserved to know what the talk was about. After all, he got nothing from us he isn't bound to hear somewhere else, if he's around these parts any time at all."

The others had been listening to this exchange. "Sam," Bart Williams asked now, "you still think you might have seen him?"

Sam Reeves hesitated, and with a shrug answered, "No, I reckon not. Does seem like I'd remember for sure, someone as big as that."

"Well, *I* never seen him," Tobe Munkers said harshly. "But I got few doubts as to what he is!" And as they all looked at him he flung out a hand in an impatient gesture. "You don't really think he was just some cowpuncher riding the grubline? Hell, all you had to do was *look!* You can tell, the way a man wears his gun rig, if he's in the habit of using it."

Reeves said, frowning narrowly, "You saying his gun is for hire?"

"Already hired, if you ask me. He was heading for Dunbar, wasn't he? What business would he have there?" Tobe Munkers insisted. "Who's he come to see? None of *us!*"

"Who, then?" Bart Williams demanded. It was Lantry who supplied an answer: "You mean Frank Stroud, I guess."

Munkers heard the skepticism behind his words. "And why not? Won't be the first tough hand on Stroud's payroll; for all we know the call could have gone out for more. He's already taken our summer range. What else do you suppose the skunk is planning, once he's got himself hitched up with the Caverhills?"

Harry Lantry's mouth tightened. He didn't want to admit to similar disturbing thoughts—the rashly excitable Tobe Munkers didn't need that kind of encouragement. Instead he said gruffly, "This is no time to be making wild guesses!"

"Ain't it? Maybe it's the only good time—now before the knot's spliced and the thing is done, and Stroud's deed to the Lease has been turned over to him. And before God knows how many more gunslicks like Bonner gets brought in to stack the odds against us! Like as not the bastard was laughing to himself all the time he ate our grub—storing up everything he saw and heard, to be passed along to Stroud. I ever do find out he was spying, I think I could kill him myself. I don't care how good he might be with that gun!"

"Brave talk," Bart Williams commented drily. "It ain't much help to us right now."

Munkers' bony cheeks grew red but he wouldn't rise to the prodding. "Nothing's going to help us," he snapped, "unless we find the guts somewhere to help our own selves. Will somebody tell me just what the hell we're doing up here, anyway—wasting the time that's left us, in trying to chase a last few miserable steers out of the timber?"

"Wait a minute!" Harry Lantry broke in. "I seem to remember, you're the one who's been saying you didn't favor leaving a single head for Stroud to make off with."

"All right, what if I said it?" the other snapped. "I got a right to change my mind. All at once it's plain to me, we're damned fools to stand by and let everything we have be took from us, piecemeal."

In spite of himself, Sam Reeves seemed impressed by the man's fiery language. "How would you say to stop it?"

"I ain't saying I know. But we can drop *this* foolishness, get the rest of the boys together and try to find something better to be doing before it's too late."

"It's already too late," Harry Lantry said; but even as he did he could sense that these men, who usually listened to him, were all at once listening to Tobe Munkers instead.

Chapter II

The trail he was following dropped Bannister off that narrow flat where the strays were being held, and onto the bench that he took to be the heart of the Holbrook Lease. He could understand even more clearly the resentment and distress of Lantry and the others at having lost out here. It looked like excellent summer range, not only for itself but also because it gave a man's herd access to those sheltered timber pockets higher up the mountain. Even without a closer look at the Wishbones, across the valley, it was easy to believe they were not going to find anything there to compensate for it. Losing their summer range, they could end up losing everything.

But Bannister had his own problems, complicated now by some of the things he had learned back there at the fire; and these began more and more to weigh on him, driving other concerns from his mind while he continued to work his way down to lower country.

The trail, obviously employed to move stock between this bench and the valley below, was easier to follow now. It took him through a break in a shallow fault scarp and, for some distance, beside a creek that was a flashing stream of snowmelt tumbling down the mountainside. Later, as the slope gentled off approaching the level of the valley floor, the trail swung gradually south. It became a wagon road that picked a looping course and gave him glimpses of a river, flowing brown and turgid between cottonwood and willow and rock banks. A couple of times he saw a wink of sunlight on shake roof or window glass or fence wire; he judged those to mark the headquarters of scattered ranches.

And then a dip round the curve of a hill brought him, without warning, into view of a really impressive cattle spread. Bannister reined in to study it. Almost directly below him, with the sweep of the river just beyond, it was well equipped and clearly prosperous—generous pastures under wire, a battery of working corrals, an impressive array of buildings. The ranch-house itself sat apart, two-storied and capacious, its square box shape broken by a veranda that extended across its front and two sides. The house had been recently painted, a dazzling white with a green roof; from here, everything looked to be maintained in first-rate condition.

There could hardly be many ranches of such size in the neighborhood, and Jim Bannister deliberated no more than a moment or two before making a decision. He could be in luck, he thought—this might be a chance of saving time and perhaps even avoiding the town itself. . . .

On the impulse he changed his course and struck toward the ranch buildings, coming in across swells of grass and through scattered pine.

Three men stood partly within the shadow of a barn entrance, examining a horse that seemed to have a lamed foreleg. They looked around as they heard a rider enter the yard, and when he aimed directly for the house one instantly left the group and came striding across the hoof-packed dirt, apparently to intercept him. Bannister arrived first and drew rein before the veranda steps, where he eased over to a more comfortable seat in the saddle while he waited.

The man looked about forty—muscular, well built. He was bareheaded, his scalp beginning to show through thinning sandy hair, and the afternoon sun shining in his face put a squinting scowl on him as he approached with his head tilted to one side. Scowling or not, he had the kind of strongly molded jaw and cheekline that gave a man a look of authority. The words he threw at the stranger were almost a challenge. "You want something?"

Rather put off by his manner, Bannister made his answer equally curt and brief. "Maybe. Am I right that this is the Caverhill place?"

"You ain't wrong," the man agreed. "I'm Wes Niles—foreman. Or, maybe it's Arch you're looking for?"

"Neither one of you, actually," Bannister said.

"If it's possible, I'd like a word with Caverhill's niece. That is, if she's around."

The other's manner underwent an alteration. His glance narrowed, became sharp with suspicion as he said, "I don't think I ever seen you. You a friend of Emily's?"

"We haven't met, that I know of."

"Then what do you want with her?"

Answering, Bannister became as coldly challenging. "I'll have to explain that to her."

The two men studied each other, over a wall of guarded reticence. "It would have to be something damned important," Wes Niles said finally. "Things are pretty busy around here. Maybe you hadn't heard—we're getting ready for a wedding on Sunday."

Bannister nodded. "I heard." He added, "My business with her is important enough."

"How do I know that? Why should I let you bother her if you can't even give me a clue?" But then, seemingly on the point of a blunt refusal, the man changed his tone and said reluctantly, "Well, I suppose I can tell her. What's the name?"

Bannister gave the same one he had used on the mountain. Niles nodded curtly. "All right, Bonner. But I won't promise anything." He ignored Bannister's nod of thanks, heeling about and going up the steps with the direct, no-nonsense stride that appeared characteristic of him.

As the man disappeared inside the house, Jim Bannister got down and stood with the dun's reins in his hand while he had a longer look around him. He could see the pair at the barn watching him. He returned their stares boldly and broke that up—one led the horse inside and the other started off toward the bunkhouse, but he had a feeling he was still being observed.

People hereabouts, he thought, either didn't see strangers often, or were simply suspicious of them.

The minutes stretched out as he stood there in the sun. The horse shifted its hoofs as though it began to feel some of Bannister's growing impatience. Niles, he was thinking, had taken time enough to deliver a dozen messages. Bannister hooked the reins over his arm, got out tobacco and papers and rolled a smoke. He got it lit and had had a couple of drags at it, when the screen door opened and the foreman was back.

Arms akimbo, Wes Niles looked down at him from the head of the steps. "Emily says she's able to give you a minute or two, but no more. Come along." He gave an impatient, summoning jerk of the head. Bannister nodded, dropped his cigarette and put a boot on it. He delayed only long enough to make a quick tie with the reins to a post of the veranda railing; after that he went up the steps and Niles turned and opened the screen for him.

They entered a hall that was too dark, after the full blast of the sun, for the visitor to make out more than a dull gleam of hardwood flooring and, at the end, the sweep of a staircase rising to upper regions. On the right, a wide archway opened; Niles pointed and said, "In there." Bannister went through, instinctively ducking his head though ceiling and archway were high enough not to give even him any trouble. He had removed his hat; he stood with it in his hand, and looked upon a friendly and well-furnished living room.

Most ranchhouses were indisputably male, equipped for hard use, with ugly leather-bound furniture and, like as not, mounted animal heads on the walls, racks of firearms, perhaps a saddle thrown into a corner. This one however looked as though a woman had had something to do with its decorating: There were curtains and drapes at the windows, the chairs and sofa were slip covered, the center table had a runner and a bowl of summer flowers and a lamp with a painted shade. Above the stone fireplace hung a painting of fruit spilling out of a basket. Everywhere was color and brightness.

A woman stood with her back to the mantelpiece, silently watching Bannister. Her yellow dress, with flounces at the waist and shoulders, nearly matched the color of her hair. He had an impression of enormous blue eyes, staring at him from a face that looked young and—to his view—remarkably pale. Her hands were clasped in front of her and he had a distinct impression that she pressed them tight to keep them from trembling.

Jim Bannister advanced toward her, aware that Wes Niles had followed him into the room and taken up a post to one side of the archway— apparently he had no intention of leaving the girl alone with this stranger. Bannister could see her look past him, as though appealing to the foreman for support. As Jim Bannister came to a halt beside the center table facing her, she brought her eyes back to him and said, in a voice that sounded tight with strain, "I understand you were asking for me . . ."

He found it possible to feel a little sorry for her, at the same time that anger was beginning to have its way with him and roughened his tone. "You're Emily Caverhill?" he demanded, and waited for her hesitant nod. "I suppose I've come at a bad time. You're being married—on Sunday, I understand. You have my congratulations."

Now she was fingering a pleat of her skirt, with nervous movements. "Thank you, Mr. . . . Bonner? That was the name, wasn't it?" And at his nod: "Have we met before somewhere?"

"No, I'm quite sure we haven't."

The girl looked past him again, toward Wes Niles standing silent by the door. She drew a breath. "And what did you want to see me about?"

"You haven't any idea at all?"

"No." She shook her head. "None at all. Should I have?" The eyes in her pallid face looked enormous; for all her dissembling, they were plainly filled with fright.

Bannister suddenly lost his patience. Swinging away from her, he said heavily, "Niles, hasn't this game gone far enough? Emily Caverhill is a woman nearly thirty years old—and this girl could hardly be out of her teens!"

He saw Wes Niles glaring at him, saw the look of fury that darkened the man's face and twisted his mouth. But he was not really prepared for the sudden move that brought the foreman's pistol out of holster and leveled its black muzzle at his chest. "Just be careful, mister!" Niles said harshly. "Get rid of that gunbelt . . ."

For a moment, Bannister could only stare; somehow it hadn't occurred to him the man would go so far. The girl, too, was startled. She exclaimed in a shaking voice, "Wes! What are you going to do with him?"

"I ain't made up my mind," the foreman told her. "But right now I want his gun."

There was no arguing with a leveled revolver. Not yet afraid, but chagrined at the predicament he had got himself into, Jim Bannister dropped his hat to the table beside him, worked the prong

34

of his belt-buckle and let belt and gun-heavy holster thump solidly on the floorboards at his feet. He stood waiting then as Niles came toward him, alert for any move. The man gave the shellbelt a boot that sent it sliding safely out of reach; Bannister stood and met his stare coldly, without letting his own reveal any trace of the alarm he actually felt.

The girl was twisting her hands together, in real distress. "I'm sorry," she exclaimed. "Wes, I tried to do just like you said. I really tried!"

"I know," Miles assured her gruffly, over his shoulder. "Wasn't your fault, Margie—you done your best. But now, run along and leave this to me."

Margie started to say something further, but checked herself. She looked at the two men uncertainly, gnawing at her lip, her cheeks still pale; then, abruptly, she turned and left the room by another door.

Niles didn't take his eyes from the prisoner long enough to see if his order had been obeyed. Bannister shook his head. "That was a cruel business—anyone could see she was scared to death. How did you get her to go through with it, whoever she is?"

"Margie? She'd do anything for Emily Caverhill. Her mother's the housekeeper here. Margie was the only substitute I could ring in on you in a hurry."

"I must say," Bannister commented dryly, "you went to a lot of trouble to keep me from seeing the Caverhill woman."

"Emily isn't here," Niles told him. "She went into town with her uncle—so, you couldn't have seen her in any event. But I mean to find out just who the hell you are and what it is you're after. You wouldn't tell Margie, but you're going to tell *me!*"

"And if I don't?" Bannister, with a coolness he was far from feeling, looked at the gun and at the face of the one who held it. "You think you're tough, Niles. But you won't pull that trigger. Not in front of her."

It was a ruse and a desperate one, but it worked. Niles, in his fierce attention to the prisoner, seemed to have lost all track of the girl. He turned his head quickly, saying, "Margie, I told you—" Too late he must have seen he had been tricked and she was no longer in the room.

That was when Bannister hit him.

He struck at the hand that held the gun, deflecting it, and at the same time aimed a blow at the foreman's blunt jaw. Haste almost undid him. His knuckles only grazed a cheekbone. Breath exploded from Niles and he started to jerk around again, the gun rising. Bannister took a solid step forward and this time his fist caught Niles just between the eyes, with all the weight of his shoulder behind it. It landed squarely. Niles gave a groan, and his eyes turned up into his head and he fell straight backward, his knees giving way. He struck the center table. The bowl of cut flowers was swept off to shatter on the floor.

Bannister had half expected to take a bullet at point blank range, but for a wonder the gun failed to go off. He stooped quickly, snatched it from the foreman's hand and after that stood a moment waiting to see if there was any fight left in Niles. The man stirred slightly, seemed to be trying to lift himself. Then with a shudder he fell back. Jim Bannister touched him with a boot-toe—he gave limply to it, with no sign of consciousness.

Trapped breath escaped from Bannister. But there wasn't time to waste. The smash of the bowl had been startlingly loud—he thought the sound must have carried through the whole house, and no knowing who might come to investigate.

If he took Niles's word about Emily Caverhill being gone from the ranch, there was nothing more he could do here. He placed the foreman's six-gun on the table, and broken glass crunched underfoot as he stepped to retrieve his own belt and weapon. He drew on his hat and was testing the set of the revolver in its holster as he walked out through the front hall, leaving Wes Niles sprawled unmoving behind him.

Despite his urgency he moved deliberately down the veranda steps to his waiting horse. As he freed the reins, he ran a look around the yard and noticed a puncher who had just unsaddled at one of the corrals, and was crossing the yard with bridle slung over shoulder. Bannister could feel his curious stare—his rangeman's eye would have marked both man and horse as strange to him. Bannister pretended not to notice, and took his unhurried time finding stirrup, swinging up, and turning away from the veranda railing. He hoped he looked as though he had legitimate business that had been taken care of. Leaving, he kept the dun at an easy walk and tried not to show that he expected, any moment, to hear an alarm burst out behind him.

The yard seemed to stretch interminably under the white glare of the sun; seconds crawled with maddening slowness. But he held steady and no one challenged him, and presently he found himself passing through the shadow of a gate that had a wooden signboard burnt with the Caverhill brand—a spur with one broken shank—suspended from its high cross bar. Beyond, wagon tracks cut across the slope to join the main road through the valley, leading away southward. Within minutes the contour of the land dropped the ranch buildings out of sight behind him.

The road dipped briefly to cross a dry creek that at one time had tumbled out of the higher timber, but was now only an eroded bed of stones and rubble. Jim Bannister scarcely hesitated before reining aside into this. The dun's hoofs raised a clatter but would leave few prints here. After climbing a little distance, Bannister jumped his horse out of the gully and was quickly into trees that made a thin screen across the slope. Fallen needles deadening hoofsound, Bannister circled back through the timber until he found that, having dismounted, he could once more look down from cover and see what was happening in the Caverhill yard.

In this clear air he scarcely needed the field glasses he took from the case strapped to his saddlehorn. When he looked through them the buildings of the ranch leaped startlingly close and a touch of the adjustment screw brought the figures of men sharply into focus—Wes Niles, surrounded by a clot of Broken Spur crewmen as he stood bareheaded in the sun, holding the gun Bannister had taken off him.

It didn't take a lip reader to know what was going on; their excited gestures told him enough. One of the men pointed toward the gate, but after a moment's further talk Niles emphatically shook his head. Bannister guessed he had just vetoed a suggestion that the lot of them take to their saddles—perhaps Wes Niles felt too much time had already been lost, and that the stranger who defied his gun, leaving him flattened on the floor of the living room, wasn't going to run any risk of capture by staying close. In this hill country

39

even a stranger could probably lose pursuit without too much trouble.

Niles shook his head again and with a gesture of dismissal turned away, shoving his gun into the holster as though he had just now realized he was still holding it. Leaving the men talking futilely among themselves he walked over to the house.

Bannister followed him with the glasses and discovered, on the veranda, a splash of brightness that was Margie's yellow dress; the older woman beside her would be her mother, the Caverhills' housekeeper. Niles paused below them a moment, for some further words. Then, abruptly, he swung away and vanished from sight among the ranch buildings.

Slowly lowering the glasses, Jim Bannister stood there in the shadow of the trees, with the dun pawing at the ground somewhere behind him. He scrubbed a palm across his jaw and frowned, as he considered. Coming to this ranch had almost ended in disaster; but his choices had been limited and now, having tipped his hand, they were fewer than ever. Still, he thought with a shrug, there'd been no way to foresee encountering anyone like Wes Niles, or having him try to run in a substitute for Emily Caverhill.

At any rate, the damage was done and he could see nothing for it but to keep going, playing a blind hand as well as circumstances let him.

Accordingly he went back to the dun, returned the glasses to their case and mounted up; he rode with caution as he swung south again through the trees, hunting a safe place to drop once more into the town road without a risk of meeting anyone from Broken Spur.

Chapter III

There was no sign of any other horseman on the road, but he kept his gun loose in the holster and half expected at every moment to hear a rider—perhaps even Niles himself—come pounding up behind him. Even after he decided he had the trail to himself he didn't relax his wariness, and this was heightened when, presently, the valley walls narrowed and he picked up sight of buildings, crowded between steep walls that amplified the sound of rushing water.

Below this point, the valley apparently widened and played out in rolling ranch country; here, the town of Dunbar sat on a narrow flat hemmed in by the river channel and by the steep rise of rock and timber behind it, that cast it into the shadow of late afternoon. A man who had learned to avoid towns unless it was absolutely necessary, Bannister approached this one with an all too familiar tension growing in him. He passed a livery barn and corral on his left, on the flat near the river bank; otherwise the town's business establishments all stood opposite, facing the tumbling river across the wagon ruts that widened here to serve as Dunbar's main street. Among others he saw a couple of saloons, a restaurant, a general store, a barbershop, a gunsmith's and the big white block of a hotel. Behind this single line of buildings, residences occupied the space between them and the timbered rise. He noticed the spire of a church steeple, also painted white, and remembered that was where Emily Caverhill and Frank Stroud were scheduled to be married on Sunday, two days distant.

Uncertain of his moves, Bannister rode into town.

A steady wind followed him in, as though the flow of the river sucked a current of air along with it; dust ran in gritty sheets from under the dun's hoofs, and a bootmaker's wooden sign creaked as it swung from its support. He observed with narrow interest the small log-and-stone building that housed the town's jail—the sign on the adjoining marshal's office was misspelled, he noticed, with one "L" too many. Bannister passed that by, but a moment later drew rein before a general mercantile. This, from its sign, was also the post office for Dunbar, Colorado, and as such was of interest to him. He dismounted, dropping his reins across a tie-pole, and walked inside.

It was a store equipped to fill the needs of its range-country customers, its shelves and counters and bins lined and stacked and filled with a great variety of merchandise. Bannister looked around and discovered the mail window in a corner at the front, with a brass grille and letter scales and a pigeon-holed rack behind it. An old man with wisps of white hair straggling at his collar was sorting through a fistful of envelopes; he peered over his glasses as the stranger approached his window. "We're fresh out of stamps," he said curtly. "Sorry."

Bannister said, "No stamps. I was wondering if you'd have a letter for me, general delivery. The name is Bonner."

The faded stare narrowed on him, more closely. "I do, for a fact. It's been setting here close to a week." He got another clutch of mail out of a slot in the rack, riffled through it and quickly produced a fat-looking business envelope. "Denver postmark," he said. "No return address. I was beginning to wonder if anyone was ever gonna pick it up. Knew we didn't have no Bonners around these parts, and it ain't often I get mail for people I never even heard of."

"Thanks," Bannister said as it was handed through the window.

He was uncomfortably aware there was no gossip like a small-town postmaster, and he knew from the weight of his stare that this was one who would never forget his face. He stuffed the envelope into a hip pocket, as though it were nothing of any immediate interest.

"Don't ever see many strangers through here, come to mention it," the old man commented, probing. "Expect to be around awhile, Mr. Bonner? You'll find it's a good town—nice people."

"Glad to hear it," Bannister said briefly. He gave the other a nod, and got out of there as discreetly as he could.

With the reins in his hands, he considered. The dun had traveled a good many hard miles since it last had a graining, and he could never know when he might have to call on it for some unexpected, extra effort. So he swung again into the saddle and turned back along the street, ducking his head against the gritty wind that swept a strong gust against him. He crossed the deep ruts to the livery barn, standing by itself on the river bank, and rode his horse into the shadowy interior.

An unshaven figure with a gimp leg came limping out of a tack room to see what was wanted. He accepted a silver dollar for a bait of hay and oats, and appeared happy to let his customer take care of the horse himself. There was a pump beside the door. Bannister got water, stripped gear and saddle from the dun and put it in a stall where he filled the manger from a grain bin. While the horse fell to eating, he allowed himself the time to find out what was in that letter he had picked up at the general store.

The hostler had disappeared again and Bannister was alone in the hay-smelling and rustling silence of the barn. Near the rear entrance, where he heard the voice of the river in its channel and the canyon's southern wall lifting beyond, he found a seat on a bale of hay, got the envelope out and tore it open.

The letter was written on plain and unmarked stationery, without date or heading, but he recognized the rather crabbed handwriting; he did not need the letterhead of the Western Development Corporation—main office: Chicago, Illinois—or the signature of Boyd Selden rather than a single initial at the end, to tell him who had sent it. Bannister read quickly, with a frown of deep concentration.

I write this in haste, with no real assurance it will reach you. I only hope, if you actually get to Dunbar, you will remember to check the post office as was agreed, on the chance of my having further communication. And for fear this letter should fall into the wrong hands, I must be very careful how much I say.

There is new information from the P's [Bannister supplied: *Pinkertons*] that more than ever proves to me we are on the right track. They now tell me our subject left Houston some four years ago, shortly after WM [*Wells McGraw*] had left her stranded there; she came to Denver in company with another man—a second-string gambler, by all descriptions—but they soon seem to have parted company.

While here in Denver, subject appears to have learned for the first time of her uncle's existence, and somehow got in touch with him.

AC [*Arch Caverhill*] apparently accepted her almost as though she were his own daughter, instead of merely a niece. Never having married, he has no family of his own. He and his brother—subject's father, who died some dozen years earlier—had lost touch long before that. From what I gather, the father probably didn't amount to very much.

Frankly I don't know how much you can hope to accomplish in Dunbar, but again I urge you to proceed with tact and caution. These qualities, I'm afraid, are not in long supply with you. Their lack helped get you into your trouble, down in New Mexico. Naturally I can understand the terrible loss you sustained when WM came at you with his hired thugs, to threaten you into accepting the offer you'd refused for your ranch, and your wife was accidentally killed in the shooting. A most regrettable occurrence! Even so, had you tried to secure witnesses and corroborating evidence instead of simply taking off after the man you held responsible, you might have avoided much of the grief we are now trying to undo.

Of course we are not going to prove you did not kill WM; you've never denied it, in court or out. I happen to believe you when you say it was not your intention, but that when you caught up with him, he tried to trick you and in the end you had to shoot the man in self defense. Still, you were tried and legally convicted, and except for the lucky chance of a jailbreak you would have hanged months ago. And of course, life is a precious thing. I suppose you'd have to prefer being a fugitive, with your ranch lost and a noose hanging over you—to say nothing of the reward offer that the Company I work for keeps raising on the man who dared to kill one of its field agents.

Nevertheless I continue to hope. If we can just find the evidence to back your characterization of WM, and raise a reasonable presumption that your killing him was justified, there's a real chance of getting your murder conviction set aside. Because, the more I read the minutes of the trial, the clearer picture I get of that battery of lawyers the Company sent down to aid the prosecution: I can see how they were able to convince the court that the Company wasn't on trial, and to have any statement you tried to make ruled out of order. What's more, I think an unbiased judge will agree with me, once he looks at the record.

In my opinion, this Company of which I am an officer *is* on trial. I'm well aware of the way popular feeling runs against the "syndicates" in this part of the country, because of the methods they have sometimes used; I would like to prove that times are changing. In your case I obviously think you were wronged, but I admit my reasons for wanting to help rectify the matter are partly selfish: I mean to have the credit for dislodging from this organization one or two of the key men responsible for this situation, and see that it never happens again!

So, a great deal rides on your mission there in Dunbar. Of course, it may not come to anything. It may turn out the woman knows nothing at all—but, that's the gamble we take. On the other hand, if she *can* help, she just might still be resentful enough at M for making her his mistress and then abandoning her, that time in Houston.

In any case, I have to repeat a warning. You are on your own. You already know why the P's are bowing out of the case: AC is an important man, with powerful friends, and naturally I couldn't allow them to identify me as their principal if matters came to a pinch. For the exact same reason, should you get yourself in trouble there's very little I can do to help. So, watch your step!

You know my address here in Denver. I expect to be here until the middle of the month. I shall be hoping for a communication from you.

Good luck,
S.

Jim Bannister read the letter twice through, and afterward sat frowning over it for long minutes. Presently he took out papers and tobacco and built himself a smoke. His mouth and eyes were grave with thought as, using the same match, he touched off the pages of the letter one by one.

He watched them blacken and curl to nothing, and then a breath of the warm wind that blew along the canyon came through the doorway, to pick the ashes up and swirl them away.

Wes Niles rode into town and made directly for a two-storied frame building, halfway along the single line of business houses, whose lower floor contained the offices of a cow-country lawyer and land dealer. When he dismounted and tied his horse, a roan, it was toward the outside stairs slanting up the west wall of the building that Niles headed. Before climbing he paused, a hand on the railing, and put a slow look over the length of the street on the off chance of seeing the dun that the stranger at Spur had ridden.

It wasn't in evidence. He touched the place where the big fellow's knuckles had struck him, on the solid frontal bone just over the bridge of the nose; and he winced and swore a little, thinking sourly and not for the first time that he was going to be lucky not to get a couple of black eyes out of it. As it was there was a definite, dull ache behind his forehead. He could only hope the sonofabitch had cracked a knuckle giving it to him.

Scowling, he climbed the steps, rapped twice on the door at the head of them, and tried the knob. It opened under his hand, and he walked into the musty little room that served Arch Caverhill as a town office.

Ensconced in his padded swivel chair, behind a scarred and battered expanse of desk, the boss of Broken Spur had pen in hand and was checking figures in a ledger. He looked up as his foreman entered. He was in shirtsleeves and waistcoat; his coat and the white, low-crowned planter's hat which was his only affectation hung on a coat tree in the corner behind him.

Keen brown eyes, deep beneath white thickets of brows, peered at Wes Niles and seemed to read something in his manner. "Yes?" the rancher demanded.

Before answering, Niles has a quick look about the room. It was sparsely furnished—an old horsehair sofa against one wall, where he suspected his boss sometimes took an afternoon nap as the first symptoms of old age began to make themselves felt; a couple of chairs, a wooden file case crammed with ledgers and papers and with an untidy pile of old stock journals heaped on its top. There was no other occupant and Niles said, unnecessarily, "Emily ain't around, I guess."

The older man shook his head. "I left her at Mrs. Claypool's—more fussing to be done with that wedding dress. You'd think they'd have it fitted by now. But, I reckon women have to have such things just so, and time's getting short. If you want to see her, you best wait. It's no place for a man to be messing in."

"I just wanted to be sure she wasn't here," Niles said, and closed the door behind him as he came quickly to the desk. "Arch, I'm afraid there's bad news."

"Oh?" Caverhill laid down his pen and pushed the ledger away. "Let's have it, then," he said crisply.

There was never any formality between these two. Wes Niles dropped onto a straight chair

53

beside the desk, placed his sweated black Stetson on his knee, and said without preliminary, "A stranger showed up at the ranch this afternoon, looking for Emily. Said his name was Bonner, but he wouldn't tell me what he wanted. All he did say was, they'd never met." Seeing his boss's frown the foreman wagged his head as he added, "You and I have been wondering all along when something like this was going to happen."

"What did he look like?" Arch Caverhill demanded.

"Big fellow—yellow-haired. No brand on his horse. He wore a gun like he knew how to use it. . . ."

"Bonner . . ." The old man repeated the name. "She ever mention the name to you? Or anyone that might fit his description?"

"No." Niles suggested, "No reason, I guess, why we couldn't just come right out and ask her."

"*You* ask her. Whatever you do, leave me out of it. Last thing we can afford is for Emily ever to know how much you've passed on, of the things she told you."

"Of course."

Caverhill had a nose like the blade of an ax, and a habit of stroking it with thumb and forefinger when he was sorely beset and thinking hard about something. He rubbed it now and his fierce old eyes, beneath the thickets of bristling brows, peered at his foreman.

The latter shifted uncomfortably in his chair, having more to tell and reluctant to. "Maybe you'll think I done a fool thing, Arch," he went on gruffly. "But it occurred to me, if he *thought* he was talking to Emily he might spill enough to show what he'd come for. Anyway, I made the try: I got Margie Ryland to put on her best dress and pretend to be her. Only, this Bonner never fell for it—Margie was pretty nervous, and anyway he seemed to know she couldn't be old enough." He added defensively, "Hell, I still figure it was worth a try."

Caverhill neither argued nor agreed. "So what happened when he caught on?"

"Why, he left. He—" Niles hesitated, and embarrassed color began to spread up through his cheeks, even darkening the faint discoloration of bruise on his forehead. "I guess I have to tell it all," he grunted. "Fact is, I sort of lost my head. I tried to keep him there, to give you a chance at him. I pulled my gun—but somehow or other he managed to trick me, and he laid me out."

"With his fists?" Caverhill eyed his stocky foreman as though he could not believe it.

The other grudgingly admitted it. "Long enough to get away without anyone stopping him. Maybe it was only a lucky punch, but he sure as hell chopped me down!" And he again felt the dully aching spot, and winced.

Arch Caverhill looked down at the hands that

lay on the desk before him—callused hands, toughened and browned by the scouring of weather and ropes and the burns from many branding irons. He said slowly, "I guess you and me are both thinking the same thing. Of course, we can be wrong—we can *hope* we're wrong. But no matter what this stranger wants, it can hardly mean any good.

"And why today, of all times!" he exclaimed, and struck the desktop suddenly with a fist. "This close to Sunday . . . Damn it, Wes! We can't let him ruin everything for Emily—*now*. Not him, or anybody!"

"Sure, Arch," Niles said gruffly. "I know how it is—her being near as you'll ever come to having a youngster of your own. You think you got to make it up, for the bad life that horse tradin' brother of yours gave her and her ma. Only—"

He hesitated. "Only, what?" Caverhill demanded. And the foreman drew a breath, like a man about to unburden himself of troubling thoughts he had kept resolutely unspoken.

"I just wonder," he said. "It's none of my business, of course. But does it bother you at all, that you might be making a bad mistake?"

"Letting her marry Frank Stroud? That's what you mean, ain't it?" The old man eyed him fiercely. "It's no secret that you don't like him much. Maybe I got a few reservations of my own," he admitted. "The man strikes me as

56

ambitious, with maybe even a spot of ruthless-ness—but hell! The same's been said of *me,* most of my life. Whatever else, he's a cattleman; and that's important, because Emily and whoever she marries are going to take over Broken Spur, one of these days. Just how soon, none of us has any way of knowing."

Wes Niles put in a quick protest. "You shouldn't talk that way, Arch. You got a lot of years in you yet."

Caverhill lifted a shoulder and let it drop. "Can any man say that and be sure of it?" he retorted mildly. He picked up the pen he had been writing with and turned it between his hands, frowning. "Wes, the main point is—Frank's her choice. And since he is, by God, if only for once in her life I mean to see Emily has something she's set her heart on!"

"But could you be paying too high a price?" And at the probing look that got him, he added in explanation: "This time I'm talking about the Holbrook Lease."

"What about it?" his boss demanded. "Mrs. Holbrook's price wasn't high at all. Not a cent more than I was happy to spend on a wedding present."

"Some say it's no wedding present," Niles insisted doggedly. "They say it was Stroud's price for going through with this marriage. What's more, the word has got out somehow that you're waiting until the knot's tied before you turn the deed over to him. And they claim that's more than just a formality. They figure it for a club you're holding over his head."

"Nonsense!" But the rancher's deep-seamed cheeks had taken on spots of color, almost as though he might have been stung by some barb of truth in the charge. He looked down at the pen he was holding, seemed surprised to discover it had snapped in two in his hands. With a grunt he tossed it aside. "Who'd say a thing like that?" he demanded angrily. "I suppose it's the same soreheads that claim I stole the Lease from them: Lantry, and Reeves and them others."

"What if it is?" the foreman said. "Maybe they ain't to blame for talking sore. They'd been using that grass for a lot of summers; they'd come to depend on it. I don't think they ever really figured you'd buy it out from under their noses—and then turn it over to Stroud, that none of 'em like. It's cost you the goodwill and friendship of men you've known for years," Niles pointed out, defying the old man's piercing glare. "That's what I meant about the price being high. I haven't wanted to say this," he added. "But I figure you and me can be honest with each other."

"Any other man on my payroll," Caverhill told him, "I'd fire him for saying it to my face! Damn it, nobody has to be *bribed* into marrying my Emily!"

"I hope not," Wes Niles said bluntly. "I'll have

to admit, the idea occurred to me that Frank Stroud might have learned something of what happened to her in Denver and them other places. I was beginning to think buying the Holbrook property for him might be what it cost you, to make him go through with the marriage. I'd hate to have believed that."

"Well, it ain't so," Arch Caverhill snapped. "Now you best get the hell out of here. I'm trying to keep my temper with you, for even suggesting it!"

"I'm going." Wes Niles was already on his feet, hat in hand. At the door he turned back. "About that Bonner fellow—you leave him to me, Arch. I'll take care of him; I already owe the bastard something." And he grimaced a little at the persistent ache behind his brow.

Caverhill muttered. "All right—just don't jump to any more conclusions. We have to *know*. Once we're sure, though, that he's what we both think, I won't give much of a damn what you do to him. In my book, nothing's lower than a blackmailer!"

Their glances met—this time in complete agreement. Niles gave a tight nod. "I think some of our boys are here in town. I'll hunt them up and spread the word, so we'll be ready for him next time he shows his face—either here, or at the ranch.

"One way or another, Arch, we'll deal with him!"

Chapter IV

It wasn't at all late; the sky above the canyon was still full of light. But Dunbar, with the blocky bulk of the mountain looming over it, had already been cast into a premature dusk. A few lamps burned in a window here and there, and beyond the open double doors of the church, warm candle glow picked out the center aisle, lined with its rows of wooden pews, and the altar at the farther end.

Under a tall pine across the dusty street, Jim Bannister leaned a shoulder negligently against the rough bark, looking like a man with nowhere in particular to go and nothing better to do than roll up a cigarette while he waited for evening to settle and for the town to start tuning up. There was not much activity in this section of town just behind the one business street, and he doubted if he was conspicuous enough there in the tree shadow to draw anyone's curious attention.

He dug out a match and had it poised to light when the sound of a pump organ began across the stillness and the dust of the street; he found himself held by it, unmoving.

Bannister knew little of music, but he recognized the tune well enough; it whisked away the years and the miles, and it was as though he stood in just such another church, in another town and state, listening to that same wedding music while a girl came down the aisle toward him. Only, now the girl was dead—killed by a careless bullet; and a tortured and devious route had led him from that moment to this, only to have a remembered bit of organ music bring the past suddenly alive again in all its bitterness and poignancy. And Jim Bannister's face was grim as he snapped the match to flame on a thumbnail, and put it to the cigarette he had built.

Shaking out the match, to drop it into the dust, he saw a man and woman approaching the church along the farther walk; he guessed at once who they had to be.

The organ continued playing, while the reed-thin figure of a man in preacherly dark clothing came out to greet the new arrivals. Bannister had a moment to observe them across the width of the street, shaking hands and chatting. The white-haired man in the white planter's hat would, of course, have to be Arch Caverhill. There was a spare and energetic dignity about him; still, no one could doubt his origins—he bore too definitely the markings of someone who had spent a lifetime in the saddle.

As for Emily Caverhill, she could hardly have been more different from the girl in the Broken Spur living-room—tall, and dark of hair, and with a maturity that blonde little Margie could never hope to imitate. Wes Niles must really have been determined on a long gamble, in trying to pass one off for the other. Bannister studied her now with intent interest—this woman who represented his last possible link with Wells McGraw, and who had brought him so many miles. But even if he had finally located her, he wasn't any closer to knowing exactly what good it was going to do him.

Now the organ had ceased and three more women came out to join the group on the church steps. A couple of them looked quite young, hardly more than adolescents—Bannister, watching the exchange of greetings, wondered if they were here in the role of bridesmaids. The older woman, who might be the preacher's wife, held several sheets of music and she and Emily Caverhill began looking through them, obviously choosing numbers for the ceremony. From the impatient looks he saw directed toward the lower end of the street, and the way Arch Caverhill pulled out a watch and consulted it, Bannister guessed that they all were waiting, with the time for starting the rehearsal already past due. He was sure of this when, presently, a pair of horsemen came into view and turned up toward the church, at a leisurely pace.

The one who lifted a hand in answer to Emily Caverhill's wave of greeting was a spare, well-built figure of a man who, to Bannister's eye, betrayed a hint of vanity in the cut of his clothes and in the trappings of his saddle and riding gear. He didn't look as though he had been hurrying to get here, and he was in no hurry now. Frank Stroud gave the impression that if he was late it concerned him hardly at all—he counted it his due that others should wait for him.

He passed the tree where Bannister stood without so much as a sideward glance, but the one with him turned and gave the stranger a stabbing look that appeared to miss nothing. There was no hitch rail at the church; Stroud dismounted and flipped the reins to his companion, who caught them neatly and rode on to a vacant lot just beyond. There the trunk of a pine showed scars from many hitchings. Watching the man dismount and tie both horses, Bannister eyed the gun and belt strapped prominently about his waist, and speculated a little about Frank Stroud thinking it oddly significant that the bridegroom needed to bring a bodyguard to a wedding rehearsal.

It seemed highly doubtful that this was his choice of a best man!

There were greetings and small talk yonder on the church steps. Stroud's bodyguard—Bannister wondered if he would be the Ridge Decker he'd heard mention of, up on the Holbrook Lease— held himself aloof from all that, spinning up a cigarette as he stood beside his horse. He seemed rather more interested in the one he could see loitering under the pine tree, across the dusty street; Bannister felt the weight of his stare and debated whether it might be time for him to move on, before he aroused real curiosity.

Suddenly and without warning a body of riders came pouring into the lower end of the street. They came on purposefully until, scarcely a half block from the church, they abruptly pulled in—at Bannister's guess, having caught sight of the people there on the steps. The street lay in shadow, but enough light remained in the sky so that faces were recognizable; Bannister made out Harry Lantry and Sam Reeves and others he'd seen at the cookfire up on the Holbrook Lease.

They sat their milling horses as though uncertain as to the next move—all except one. For now, with a yell, Tobe Munkers kicked his animal and sent it leaping forward, despite a protest from Lantry and a move by someone to grab the reins. All alone he charged straight toward the church, and Bannister saw the gleam of the saddle gun as he brought it out from under his knee. "Stroud!" The name broke from him, almost a scream of rage.

For an instant it looked as though he meant to run his animal right up the steps and over the people who stood as though frozen, watching him come. But at the last possible instant Munkers pulled his horse in and then he was tumbling out of the saddle, yelling Frank Stroud's name a second time. He hit the ground spraddle-legged but his own forward momentum threw him heavily to his knees. The rifle fell from his hand into powder-dry dust. He seemed to search for it, crouched there on all fours; then he was scrabbling at the weapon, grabbing it up as he fought his way unsteadily to his feet.

It was in that instant that Bannister saw Tobe Munkers was staggering drunk.

That wasn't all he saw. Yonder, near the tied horses, Stroud's bodyguard had drawn his belt gun and now he was coming at a quick prowl, closing in. Bannister didn't think anyone else had noticed—certainly not Tobe Munkers himself, who was standing there in the dust, visibly weaving on his legs as he bawled incoherent curses at Frank Stroud and brandished his rifle. Apparently he could see that Stroud wasn't armed, at least openly, and he appeared oblivious to any danger coming up from another direction.

Bannister's own instinct was to stay completely out of this—certainly, he owed Tobe Munkers nothing; but it looked as though no one else was going to make any gesture to stop it. Somehow, almost without thinking, he found himself moving forward across the empty street. He came up on Munkers from the blind side, easily out-distancing Stroud's man. He said, "This has gone far enough."

Tobe Munkers wheeled about, his boots almost tangling. His face looked flushed and his eyes a little blurred, but he plainly wasn't too drunk to recognize someone he had already marked for an enemy. "*You!* Stay clear of me!" he shouted thickly, and the barrel of the saddle gun lifted.

Bannister's palm struck the weapon, knocking it aside even as the other tightened on the trigger. He hadn't seen Munkers work the lever and hoped it wouldn't go off. It did, however. There was a jolting rush of gases through the metal tube beneath his hand; the shot lashed upon the street quiet and drew a stifled shriek of fright from one of the women on the nearby church steps.

Reaction made Bannister pull in his gut, on a quick, indrawn breath, but it was pure, white-hot anger that tightened his grip on the barrel of the weapon; he wrenched it free. Munkers let it go, but next moment he was groping to pull the rubber-butted handgun from his belt.

Bannister didn't give him time. He flung the rifle away and, not attempting to clear his own revolver, simply swung his fist. He got a better shot at the target this time than he had earlier with Wes Niles in the living room at Broken Spur; his blow took Munkers squarely on the point of his stubbled lantern jaw. Munkers' teeth clicked together, and he was spun half way around and dropped solidly. Bannister stood and looked down at him, shaking the fingers that stung a little after being forced to deliver a second knockout blow in one afternoon.

For that first moment, with the echo of the rifle in their ears, everyone on the scene appeared stunned by what had nearly happened. The horse Munkers had ridden, after wheeling and pitching a little and stirring up the acrid street dust under its hoofs, had swung back to rejoin its friends in the group of riders from the Holbrook Lease, and one of those men had presence of mind to seize the flying reins and drag it in. That seemed to break through whatever was holding them; Jim Bannister, sensing trouble, quickly dropped a hand to his own holstered gun.

He said sharply, "Lantry, keep them back! Your man isn't hurt, but it's a wonder. He could have got himself killed."

"Yes—why *didn't* you kill him?" the one named Sam Reeves retorted fiercely. "It's no more than we could have expected from you!" Bannister looked into the distorted features of the man, saw the hatred in his pale-lashed eyes and found it mirrored in other faces. And realized clearly, then, that none of them understood.

Probably they hadn't even seen that gunman closing in, had no idea why Bannister had made his move. As far as they could see, he had merely confirmed Tobe Munkers' claim that this stranger must be another gun for Stroud's payroll; and in their present mood there was probably little use in trying to set them straight. Bannister shrugged and let it go.

He turned then as Frank Stroud and Arch Caverhill came down the steps of the church and out into the street. On closer view they confirmed Bannister's earlier impressions: Caverhill, a man weathered and tempered by time, the other still in his thirties but with a natural hardness about him. Stroud, he thought, exuded competence and the arrogant sureness of someone who had tested his strength and was pleased with the results. He was undeniably a handsome figure of a man, tall—almost as big as Bannister himself—and rangily built. His hair and mustache were full and dead black. The eyes that touched Bannister were black also and, he thought, completely cold.

Stroud looked at the limp body in the dirt. He prodded it with a polished boot-toe and it gave limply. "Which one is this?" he demanded in a tone that held a note of contempt.

Arch Caverhill answered him. "His name's Tobe Munkers."

"Well, I knew it had to be one of them." Stroud lifted his stare, then, to the group of horsemen. Harry Lantry had dismounted and taken a step to join the men around Munkers' body; but he halted when Stroud demanded harshly, "Did the lot of you put him up to this? Did you draw straws to decide who'd have the pleasure of killing me?"

"Tobe was drinking," Lantry retorted stiffly. "He never could manage his likker."

"Then, if he'd blown Frank Stroud's head off," Caverhill suggested, "do you mean nobody should have held him to blame?" He shook his gaunt, white-maned head. "Harry, I expected better of you!"

Visibly stung, Lantry's face darkened. "All I meant was, we none of us had any inkling what was in his head. It happened too fast; we couldn't stop him."

"He can damn well be thankful *somebody* stopped him!" Caverhill said. "Because otherwise it would have been murder. It's plain enough you all had mischief in mind, or you wouldn't even be here—whether or not you actually planned to gun down my girl's intended, right in front of her eyes! So don't think the rest of you wouldn't have had something to answer for!"

"Arch, I swear—!" But Harry Lantry bit off his protest, unfinished, as though he saw no use in it.

Caverhill was already turning his attention to the one who had put Tobe Munkers out of action. He had to tilt his head to look up at the stranger. Brows drawn in a puzzled frown above his fierce beak of a nose, he told Bannister, "These men seem to know you, but I don't think *I've* ever seen you before. I'm Arch Caverhill. Whoever you may be, I got to say you moved fast and you moved well. I think we're in your debt, Mister—"

He was probing for a name, and the stranger let him have one. "Bonner. Jim Bonner . . ." He continued, "I just happened to see what was going on, from across the street. It seemed the proper thing to step in and try to head it off."

"Umm . . ." The old man was pawing at that crooked beak of a nose with one bent forefinger; the skin about his eyes, dried to parchment and burnt brown by many suns, was pinched into narrow creases as he studied the stranger before him. Something about his expression touched Bannister like a cold warning. Maybe, he thought, the old cowman had already talked to his foreman, had learned from him about a man who called himself Bonner, and who had talked his way into the living room at Broken Spur and there confronted the bogus Emily Caverhill. . . .

Whatever else Caverhill might have said was lost, then, as a newcomer suddenly walked in on the scene. He had come up from somewhere at a quick and reaching stride, his arms swinging . . . a narrow-waisted man, with a town marshal's badge pinned to his unbuttoned vest. The face above the badge was stern, the mouth a thin line, the man's hair and neatly trimmed beard salted with gray—Bannister judged him at close to fifty.

He looked at Tobe Munker, who was beginning to stir and groan a little; he ran a quick appraising look around the faces of the others. "Mr. Caverhill," he said, with what Bannister took to be a certain amount of deference, "what's happening here? What was the gunshot I heard?"

The old man seemed suddenly loath to have the law involved in something he apparently saw as a private matter. "It's nothing serious, Merl," he said, shaking his head briefly. "And it's been settled."

"I'd call it serious," Frank Stroud declared, contradicting him. "Here's a man tried to put a bullet in me. Anyone could see I'm unarmed, which makes it a deliberate attempt at murder. He, and these friends of his, seem to think they have some sort of grievance."

The marshal looked thoughtfully at the men grouped in back of Harry Lantry. "I've heard some talk to that effect," he agreed, noncommittally. He turned then and his cold stare settled on Bannister. "I don't think I know this man."

"He took the rifle away from Munkers," Caverhill answered quickly, "and almost got shot doing it. He's a stranger to me—says his name is Bonner."

The lawman repeated the name, half to himself, thoughtfully. Caverhill completed the introductions. "Bonner, this is Merl Blackman—he's our law, here in Dunbar."

Bannister nodded, not liking at all the unwavering look that rested on him. Then an angry question from Frank Stroud broke in.

"Well? You've heard the story, Blackman. What's the law going to do about it?"

"The law?" Merl Blackman echoed him, and the cold weight of his stare shifted to Stroud. "Sounds to me you're terribly concerned about legalities, all at once. I see Ridge Decker standing there," he added, with a nod toward the silent gunman. "From all I've heard, he's your personal bodyguard—to put a polite name to it! So I'm a little surprised you'd call on the law for help. Or, for that matter, let some total stranger save your neck for you!"

The thinly veiled sarcasm sunk home. Bannister saw a slow flush of anger spread up through Stroud's dark features, and yonder Ridge Decker's head rose sharply as he glared at the lawman. Merl Blackman didn't wait for an answer. Just at that moment the man in the dust at their feet, who had been rapidly regaining consciousness, let out a groan and with a convulsive movement pushed to a sitting position. Hands flat against the ground to brace him, he brought his head up and put a blank and wavering look over those he found clustered about him.

The marshal leaned to pluck the gun out of Munkers' belt holster, and shove it behind his own waistband. He also picked up the fallen rifle, dust dripping from it. Then, having cornered Tobe Munkers' weapons, he said bruskly, "All right—on your feet!" and he hooked the man under an arm and without ceremony hauled him up.

Munkers stood up, staggering and protesting. "Lemme go!" he shouted. "What do you think you're doing?"

"I'm taking you to jail," Blackman told him.

"No!" The man tried boozily to strike out, to pull free of the hand that gripped him. "I won't go!"

"The hell you won't!"

And the marshal gave him a shaking that made the head wobble on his shoulders and left him limp, the fight taken out of him. As though only then remembering Emily Caverhill and the other women, watching from the church doorway, Blackman turned to them and said gruffly, "I hope you ladies will excuse my language."

Arch Caverhill seemed to be having second thoughts. He suggested now, "The man's had time to cool off. Maybe it isn't absolutely necessary to—"

"I think it is," the marshal said. "For his own good, and as an object lesson to the rest of them. I'm taking him in." The shaking may have cleared some of the whiskey fumes out of Tobe Munkers' head; some of the belligerence seemed to have left him. At least he offered no further resistance when the marshal turned him and pointed him downstreet, and gave him a prod. "Move along, now."

As the prisoner stumbled into motion, Merl Blackman let his flat stare rest briefly on Jim Bannister. The latter steeled himself to meet it. It was always an uncomfortable moment, when someone with a badge pinned on his waistcoat seemed to show undue interest in him; though his likeness on the reward dodgers he had seen wasn't a good one, the description that accompanied it had been all too accurate.

But the lawman turned away, dismissing him, and Bannister could breathe again.

Hustling the prisoner ahead of him, Merl Blackman all at once found himself confronted by Tobe Munkers' friends: he was brought to a halt as Sam Reeves swung his horse broadside, deliberately barring the path. Blackman could have gone around, but instead he met the challenge directly, with upflung head and icy stare. This lasted only for moments. Then Harry Lantry said a word or two, sharply, and ended what could have turned into something serious.

Reeves swore, and yanked the reins to pull aside. The lawman and his prisoner walked through the ranks of the horsemen, in dead silence except for the sound of their boots stirring up the dust.

Bannister thought Harry Lantry would have liked to continue the discussion, but Caverhill, and the others in front of the church, already seemed to have forgotten him. After an irresolute

75

moment Lantry gave it up. He swung away with a shake of the head, found stirrup and lifted into the saddle, moving like a very tired and discouraged man. He turned his mount and rode off down the street at a slow walk, and his companions fell in behind him; it was as though the common impulse that brought them here had been effectively blunted, at least for now.

Then they were gone, and as far as Jim Bannister could see that put an end to the matter.

Chapter V

As dusk continued to deepen, turning the sky overhead the color of steel, the church interior behind its open doors seemed to glow even more warmly with candlelight. A wind of early evening was stirring the trees that lined the street, bringing a hint of chill down off the mountain.

Frank Stroud had walked over to speak to Emily Caverhill; now Arch Caverhill approached Jim Bannister, and with the first words he spoke he seemed to have undergone a surprising change of manner. Earlier, it had held wariness and hard suspicion, but as he offered a rope-scarred hand his voice was completely cordial.

"Well, Bonner," he said, "I don't know you, but it's clear we all owe you our thanks. Whoever you are, we're lucky you've got a cool head on your shoulders."

"No reason to thank me," Bannister said as they shook hands briefly. "Just because I happened to be handy—and stuck my nose into what was none of my business."

"All the same; you saved what should be a pleasant moment from being turned into a tragedy! As you may have guessed," Caverhill added, "we're rehearsing a wedding here. I'd like you to meet our parson, Mr. Bonner. This is the Reverend Quigley . . . and Mrs. Quigley . . ."

Bannister found himself shaking hands with a rather horse-faced individual and touching hatbrim politely to his wife—the flat-chested woman who hugged her sheaf of organ music and appeared still upset by the things that had been happening. "And my niece," Arch Caverhill went on, and turned to call, "Emily . . ."

She came toward them, Stroud at her elbow. Bannister could only hope he managed to mask his true reaction to this long-awaited meeting.

First impressions could have been colored by what he knew about her; still, Emily Caverhill seemed very much like someone who guarded her thoughts. She would almost have been a beautiful woman, he thought, if it weren't for the hint of secretiveness that shadowed her eyes. When her uncle made the introductions she only nodded and said briefly, "Thank you for what you did, just now."

Bannister made some kind of answer, and nodded to Stroud as Arch Caverhill finished the introductions. The old man continued, "I have a little something arranged for this evening, in the private dining room at the hotel—a supper party, following the rehearsal. I'll take it kindly to have you join us, Bonner."

"I wouldn't want to do that," Bannister protested quickly. "I'd feel like an intruder . . ."

"Nonsense! I really insist. It's the least we can

do to thank you. It's at eight o'clock, you hear? We'll count on you." Caverhill was clearly a man who expected to have his way.

Even so, Bannister would still have refused out of a sense of propriety. But then, as he looked at the woman it struck him that this might be the chance he'd been hoping for. He had come here to Dunbar with no other purpose than somehow to meet Emily Caverhill; he might never have as good an opportunity. And so Jim Bannister nodded and told her uncle, "All right—if you put it that way."

"Fine! Fine!" exclaimed Caverhill. And the matter was settled.

Given a choice, in his present state of mind, Wes Niles would have been starting to get drunk, about now, with every intention of staying that way until Monday morning; instead, from a sense of duty he was holding himself to a single beer. He stood at one end of the bar in the biggest of Dunbar's three saloons, with the schooner in front of him and with a curtain of ill-humor surrounding him that warned other men away. He was nursing the beer, making it last, oblivious to everything else while he worked at his own particular problems.

When new arrivals in the saloon brought excitement with them, he paid no attention at all until a name he half-consciously registered turned him suddenly alert. His head lifted as one newcomer said, "It's the truth! Munkers is setting in jail, right this minute. What we heard, he was trying to murder Caverhill and Stroud and the preacher, and everybody else there at the church!"

"Tobe Munkers?" someone else exclaimed, disbelieving.

"It's what we heard. Well, he always was a wild man. . . ."

Niles was not one to chase bar-top rumors, but this was one he could not afford to ignore. He finished off his beer in a couple of swallows, snatched his hat off the counter where he had laid it, and got out of there.

In the dusk that flooded the canyon now, he could see quite a crowd gathered at the jail but he turned in another direction. He had gone less than half a block when he was confronted by a Broken Spur puncher who told him, breathlessly, "Wes, you're wanted! Arch give me word to hunt for you and send you to him, pronto. You'll find him—"

"At the church—I know. Tell me first, is anybody hurt?"

"Oh, you heard about the shooting? I guess it didn't come to anything much. But Arch said—"

Wes Niles had already left the man behind.

The doors of the church were closed but the pointed windows bloomed with candlelight. Niles let himself in. Ridge Decker, lounging in one of the rear pews, had come sharply alert at the door's opening. Caverhill's foreman gave the gunman a cold stare that contained his unconcealed dislike; afterward he stood with hat in hand, while he unobtrusively watched the rehearsal with an expression that could have been carved from wood.

The principals were gathered in a cluster near the altar—the groom and the bride and her uncle, and a couple of local girls who would be serving as bridesmaids. But no best man . . . Niles wondered sourly if Frank Stroud hadn't found anyone he considered good enough to stand up with him. Or maybe he'd wanted to use Ridge Decker, and Arch had balked at a hired gun. Whatever—it hardly mattered a damn to Niles, the black mood he was in as he watched what went on there before the altar.

Quigley, the minister, was giving instructions for the ceremony day after tomorrow—when people would be making their entrances, where they should stand. Only a murmur of talk reached to where Niles stood waiting. He heard one of the girls giggle at something, then quickly subside as though in embarrassment at being heard laughing out loud in church.

Now Arch Caverhill glanced toward the door and saw Niles waiting. At once, without bothering to excuse himself, Arch left the rest and came stalking up the aisle to join his foreman. He was about to speak when he read the open curiosity in Ridge Decker's stare, watching them, and with a grimace Arch touched Niles on the elbow. "Let's step outside . . ."

Shut away from the lights and sounds of the church, they faced each other in the chill dusk. Wes Niles said, "I heard there was some excitement."

"You might say that," his boss answered dryly. "That fellow Bonner—"

"*Bonner!* Do you mean he's cropped up again?"

Caverhill wagged his gaunt head. "He was right across the street, there, watching us—I'd seen him first thing when me and Emily arrived, but somehow never put it together until the trouble started." Scowling, Niles listened to an account of Tobe Munkers' frenzied behavior, and the quick work the tall stranger had made of putting an end to it. "You described him well enough," Caverhill said. "But I just never made the connection till he told me his name."

"Looks like the sonofabitch favors himself for a pretty tough boy!" Niles grunted. "But just let me get another chance at him!"

"No!" his boss said sharply. "I don't want that—not yet, anyway. It's more important that we try to find out what he's up to."

"I just might get that out of him, too."

"I think there's a better way. At least I figure it's worth a try. I've asked him to the supper I'm giving tonight—I want to see if we can get him to tip his hand."

"I don't know," Niles exclaimed dubiously. "What makes you so sure the fight with Munkers wasn't actually staged, to help him get on the blind side of you?"

"A trick by Lantry and his crowd, you mean?" Caverhill gave this some thought, but shook his head. "No, I stick to our first guess: Whoever or whatever he is, this Bonner is here on account of Emily, and not for any other reason. We've got to assume it's blackmail he wants—and give him the chance to prove it. That's a job you can help with, Wes. You, and Luke Elgin."

Niles gave a snort. "Elgin! That rumpot?"

"He's still my attorney—and I pay him enough to make him do what I tell him. It's up to you to see he understands his orders." But Wes Niles listened in growing doubt as Caverhill proceeded to explain what he had in mind.

"Arch, I don't like it!"

"I don't like it either. But it's too close to Sunday—we can't let anything go wrong now. I won't draw an easy breath till this Bonner situation is settled, one way or another!

"You've got your instructions," Caverhill added bruskly, overriding his foreman's resistance. "Find Luke Elgin and tell him what he's to do. Right now I got to get back in there and get straight on all this marching up and down that's expected of me, day after tomorrow. If I wasn't doing it for Emily, damned if I'd put up with such nonsense!"

As Caverhill opened the door, light from within picked out the strong, bony structure of the other man's face. The foreman nodded shortly. "All right," Niles said gruffly. "I'll find Elgin. Let's hope he's sober enough to get his lines straight!"

A little short of eight o'clock, Jim Bannister put the dun horse into a tangled thicket just behind the hotel and tied it there. The sky was still light, but here in the canyon darkness was complete; the town was quiet. As he stood beside his horse, testing to try and learn if anyone might have been observing him, Bannister distinctly heard the voice of the river in its channel, against the canyon's opposite wall.

Finally satisfied, he slipped out of the dark trees and a few minutes later was mounting the steps to the hotel veranda.

It was easily the biggest building in town, dominating this corner of Dunbar's one business street—a great, blocky slab of a structure, ablaze with lights. Wooden pillars supported a gallery across its front; oil lamps burned on either side of the lobby entrance.

He hesitated for just an instant before he stepped inside. Not knowing what he might be walking into, he had to admit to a degree of uneasiness. At least he should look presentable enough. After the unaccustomed luxury of a hot bath and shave at the town's barber shop, he had broken out a clean shirt from the spare belongings in his saddle roll. The dust was knocked from his clothing, his boots rubbed up with a rag.

The one thing that really bothered him was the gun.

He had it shoved behind his waistband, well over on the left side where it was concealed by the natural hang of his coat, but where the fingers of his right hand could easily reach it. He considered it hardly proper to go armed to a formal supper, but to be without a gun was out of the question. He could only hope some stiffness in his movements wouldn't betray the weapon digging into his ribs.

As he entered, a hum of voices, and the clatter of dishes and silverware, indicated the public dining room adjoining the lobby. But this was probably not the one he wanted; he asked the desk clerk and was directed down a hallway, to a smaller room where he found bright lamp glow ashine on a white-clothed table and glinting from the facets of cut glass and the surface of chinaware and silver. He was met by the voice of Arch Caverhill saying, "Ah! Here he is. Now we can all get started . . ."

There were to be eight at table—besides Bannister and the Caverhills and Stroud, the minister and his wife had been invited, and the two bridesmaids. These were the Misses Johnson, daughters of one of the town's merchants. Bannister, seated between them, at once found himself the center of a rivalry that lasted all through the meal, each of the sisters doing her best to monopolize him. Since both were tremendously curious he had an uncomfortable time of it, evading their efforts to learn everything they could about him. He parried their questions as best he was able, sweating a little. Still, the food was good; Bannister attacked it with the appetite of a man who had missed meals in the past and never knew when he might again.

More than once when he glanced across the table, it was to find Arch Caverhill's stare resting on him, as though in speculation. This caught him up, and touched him with alarm as he wondered again just what the man could have had in his mind, inviting a total stranger to the intimacy of a wedding supper. It baffled him, and for that reason it bothered him too. . . .

The mealtime passed. Caverhill kept the talk steered to inconsequentials, and rather pointedly away from any mention of the incident with Tobe Munkers. They were halfway through dessert, when the parson fetched up a gold watch from his pocket, snapped open the lid, and exclaimed, "My word, it's nearly nine thirty! I gave a solemn promise I'd have these girls home. Isn't it amazing how one can lose track of the time?"

That broke up the evening. Despite every protest from the Misses Johnson, the parson couldn't be budged from delivering them to their parents, forthwith. There was an exchange of good-byes and a flurry of departures, with the young ladies vying to see which could have the final word with the tall stranger and keep hold of his hand the longest. Jim Bannister was mightily relieved to see them go.

Afterward he felt it was also time for him to excuse himself but Arch Caverhill would hear none of it. "Sit down—sit down," he ordered gruffly, flapping a hand at Bannister. "We haven't had our after-dinner coffee yet. Besides, there ain't been a chance even to get acquainted." So Bannister sat down again, aware at every movement of the gun digging into him under the coat.

Watching as Caverhill refilled everyone's coffee cup, he observed again how clearly the rancher bore the mark of one who had earned his wealth, through years of the roughest kind of outdoorsman's life—a life in the saddle, bucking the worst extremes of bad weather; he was reminded somehow of old Harry Lantry. Hard years had worked on them both, fined them down and darkened their skins and turned their palms horny with callus. And yet, there was a difference. For Arch Caverhill carried the evidences of his success; while Lantry, toward the close of life, was still at the bottom of the heap, still struggling. . . .

Caverhill said with a knowing grin, "Well! You seemed to make quite a hit with the young ladies."

When Bannister only shrugged, Frank Stroud commented dryly, "It comes of his being male, and unspoken for. Or at least that was *their* impression." The cold, black stare prodded the stranger. "Actually, nobody here knows much of anything definite about you, Bonner."

"Maybe there isn't much to know," Bannister said.

"I wonder . . ." Stroud let the murmured comment hang, allowing the other to read what he would into it.

"You just passing through our country?" Caverhill asked in a casual tone. "Or planning to stay around?" When there was no immediate answer he went on: "If you're looking for a riding job, Frank might fix you up. Or, my Broken Spur has a full crew but I can generally find space for a good man. After all, we *are* in your debt."

"Thanks," Bannister said. "I haven't made any plans."

As though tired of sparring and getting nowhere, Frank Stroud demanded bluntly, "Where are you from, Bonner?"

The stranger put a smooth look on him. "Quite

a few places. I've covered considerable territory." He watched the other's stare narrow at the reply that told him exactly nothing.

That moment ended as a man in an ill-fitting business suit all at once appeared in the doorway. He had a paunch, and his cheeks, between graying muttonchop whiskers, showed a pattern of ruptured veins that might have been broken by too much hard liquor. He was nervously clutching a leather brief case. Arch Caverhill looked up, saw him there. "Yes, Luke?"

The newcomer cleared his throat. "Sorry to intrude, Mr. Caverhill, but I understand you want to look over this transfer agreement on the Holbrook property, before I go ahead and draw up the fair copy for your signature."

"That's right—that's right," the cattleman said bruskly. "I do for a fact." He added in an aside to Frank Stroud, "You know my attorney—Luke Elgin?" And to the lawyer: "You have the stuff ready?"

Elgin rummaged in the case and brought out some sheets of yellow paper, which he handed to the cattleman. The latter glanced over them, with an uncomprehending scowl. He shook his head impatiently. "I don't make no sense at all out of this legal palaver."

"If you like," the lawyer suggested quickly, "I can go over the document, and explain anything you don't understand."

"You'll damn well have to," Arch Caverhill agreed. "And I want Frank, here, to be satisfied. Did you bring that map to compare the boundary description?"

"Yes sir. It's right here." Luke Elgin produced it from his case and started to unfold it. Caverhill started to sweep back dirty dishes and clear a space, but then impatiently shook his head.

"Hell, this is no place to talk business." Abruptly he got to his feet, holding the yellow papers. "Charlie Unger has a cubbyhole he calls an office, just off the lobby. Since I own half interest in this hotel of his, he can hardly object if we borrow it for a few minutes. Come along," he told Stroud, waggling a hand. "We need to spread these things out, so we can see what's what."

Watching Stroud, Bannister thought he saw a sudden flash of suspicion work across the man's face, as he looked first at Caverhill and then at the lawyer. But with a shrug he pushed back his chair and rose. Caverhill turned to his niece. "This shouldn't take but a minute or two. Emily girl, you keep Mr. Bonner company. Talk about the weather. Have some more coffee or something. We'll try not to be long."

Emily Caverhill merely looked at her uncle, without expression. Caverhill was already ushering Stroud and the lawyer ahead of him to the door. There, Frank Stroud halted long enough to let a cold, speculative glance rest for a moment on the woman he was pledged to marry, then swing briefly to the stranger.

After that they were gone, and all at once Bannister found himself alone with the person on whose account he had journeyed here, with no more than the bare hope of a meeting.

Chapter VI

For a moment neither spoke. Looking at her across the width of the cloth-covered table, and the wreckage of the meal, Bannister found himself at a loss to know where to begin—aware, too, that he probably had very little time. Debating, he watched the woman give her attention to folding and then refolding her napkin, methodically pressing the creases flat with a thumbnail. In light of what he knew about her past, he would have expected to find her coarsened by it, yet he thought now that the grim and sometimes sordid years had left little mark on her. She was still an attractive woman, even if one could hardly guess at what lay behind the mask of her unsmiling face and downcast eyes, with the faint stain of shadow beneath them.

He was trying to frame his opening words when she suddenly lifted her head and, looking at him directly, demanded, "Who are you? Why did you really come here?"

Bannister was taken by surprise. Parrying, he said, "You think I'm not telling everything?"

"You're not telling anything—not to my uncle, not to Frank. And certainly not to those girls! I watched them trying to pry information out of you. They got nowhere at all."

"I see . . ." All at once Bannister could sense that she was under tension; her lips were pale and tight-set. Since she had opened the attack, he saw no reason not to return it. "All right. You like direct questions—*I'll* ask one: When did you last see or hear from Wells McGraw?"

No answer, for a long moment. The woman was a good actress, he thought. Her eyes betrayed nothing, as they continued to probe his face; but when she spoke her voice faltered, belying her lack of control over it. "McGraw?" she repeated. "That's a man's name? I don't think I ever heard of him."

"You've heard of Houston, Texas?"

A faintly tremulous lift of her breast betrayed her but she said, levelly enough, "I was never there—if that's what you're getting at."

"I think you were." Bannister hated bearing down so heavily, but in the few minutes allowed him he could see no other voice. "You knew Wells McGraw there. I have that on the authority of the Pinkerton Agency, Miss Caverhill. I suppose you *have* heard of them?"

" 'We never sleep,' " she quoted, and raised a shoulder slightly. "But they *can* make mistakes. And I assure you this is one of them." Abruptly then she was on her feet, pushing back her chair. "I see no point in going on with this, Mr. Bonner. I've answered your question."

"You haven't told me the truth."

No sooner had the words been stung from him than he knew he had made a bad blunder; for no woman liked being called a liar. He saw the danger signals flaring in Emily Caverhill's eyes, and sudden color bloomed in her cheeks as her head lifted angrily. "You are no gentleman," she cried, "to say such a thing!"

Belatedly, he rose to face her. She was rushing ahead, the words spilling from her lips; she seemed unaware that, with each one, she betrayed herself still further. "I'm in no position to pay you blackmail, Mr. Bonner! So I suppose you'll be going to my uncle with this—this dark secret you think you've uncovered. Or if not to him, to the man I'm about to marry . . ."

Jim Bannister stared. Blackmail being the furthest thing from his own thoughts, it had simply never occurred to him that this could be her natural first reaction. He was thrown off stride and for a moment could only shake his head, appalled by the task of somehow correcting her error.

And suddenly it was too late.

The faintest sound from beyond the hall archway—a creaking of a carpeted floorboard—was all the warning he got, and all he needed. He faded back a quick couple of steps and to the right, and the gun from under his coat was in his hand when Wes Niles came lunging into the room.

"All right, damn you!" Niles challenged. His face was flushed with anger; his own revolver was trained at the place where Bannister should have been standing. Not finding him there the foreman halted abruptly. Next moment, out of the tail of his eye he must have caught a glimpse of the tall man standing almost with his shoulders against the wall, and he jerked convulsively about—only to freeze as he saw the muzzle of the six-shooter leveled at him.

"Don't try to use that gun, Niles," Bannister warned him sharply. "Get rid of it!"

The foreman was so furious that his hands trembled; his mouth twisted out of shape as with the utmost reluctance he made his fingers open and let the weapon fall at his feet. At a further signal from Bannister he gave it a boot to send it sliding across the carpet, out of sight beneath the table. "You—" he started to say, but emotion choked off his speech.

"I don't know whose idea it was," Bannister said coldly, "yours or Caverhill's, to deliberately set me up like this and see how much you could make me spill. But, it didn't work—any more than that other dumb play you tried at the ranch—"

He was interrupted by a sudden cry from Niles: "Gilson! *Get him!*" It was his only warning, but for a man of Jim Bannister's size his reflexes were sudden. He had already dropped to one knee when a new six-gun opened up from the door-way; the burst of flame, at such close quarters, was blinding and the roar of the shot punished the ears. The bullet missed. It struck the wall somewhere above Bannister's hunched shoulder, and his own shot mingled with the echoes of the first, and with the startled outcry from Emily Caverhill. The figure that had appeared in the door just as suddenly vanished.

Bannister was up at once and lunging after it. He unceremoniously elbowed Wes Niles aside and gained the opening, ready to throw another shot; but Gilson hadn't waited for it—this was no gunman, apparently, but an ordinary Broken Spur cowpuncher, without the stomach for gunplay. Bannister reached the hall in time to see him disappear in the direction of the hotel's lobby; and he was raising a yell as he ran.

Jim Bannister swore as he lowered the gun. Turning back he found the dining room swimming now in sour drifts of powder smoke; Emily Caverhill stood just as he had left her, both palms pressed to cheeks that had drained of color. But Wes Niles had flung himself to his knees and was groping under the table in an effort to retrieve his gun. At a sharp word from Bannister he swiveled about, glowering across a bent shoulder. He had to let the weapon go. Slowly he got to his feet, to stand with head shot forward, eyeing Bannister in angry hostility.

He had failed, but Jim Bannister had no better cause to feel pleased with himself: Not only had he got nowhere with Emily Caverhill, but he had to wonder if there would be any hope at all now of convincing her he meant her no harm. Meanwhile Gilson was raising the alarm—already there was a trampling of boots, and a shouting of voices from the forward regions of the hotel.

Bannister didn't have to be told that time was quickly running out. He wanted to say something more to the woman, but after another look at her he gave it up. He spun away, and went off down the hallway at a run.

A door stood open on a kitchen's steamy heat and the odors of cooking. A Chinese in a chef's hat and apron stood gawking at him; he brandished the gun in his hand and sent the cook ducking hastily back out of danger. A little farther on, the hall took a right angle turn to reveal another door, with black night showing beyond the glass. Bannister made for it without breaking stride, and was just reaching for the knob when he heard a confusion of voices and pounding of boots, approaching the other side. He managed to brake his forward momentum.

After what happened that afternoon at Broken Spur, he should have guessed that Wes Niles was wary enough to have stationed some of his men around the building, to guard against the stranger getting away a second time. The eruption of gunfire within was all it would have taken to bring them on the run.

But he had no intention of shooting his way out if he could avoid it. Near at hand a set of narrow stairs pointed to the hotel's second story. Bannister didn't hesitate, he took them at a bound, and was half way up the shadowed stairwell before he heard the door kicked open, and excited men pouring through the hallway he had just left.

By then Bannister had his gun ready and his back pressed against the wall, to make himself as little visible as possible. However, no one seemed to think about looking there. They went on at a rush, leaving one behind to guard the door; and seeing that way blocked Bannister had no choice. He turned and hurried lightly on up the stairs, and so came out on a lamplit corridor, lined with a double row of numbered doors, that split the hotel's upper story. He halted while he considered his next move.

Somewhere at the forward end, there would be another set of steps down to the lobby. He was trapped between them—or would be, as soon as those Broken Spur punchers checked with the Chinese cook and realized which way he must have gone. With engrained caution he had checked the building before he entered it and knew there was no outside stair; more often than not, the only fire escape provided for the guests of one of these cowtown hotels would be a coil of rope they could throw down from a window in an emergency.

That at least suggested an idea. He started trying doors, but every one seemed to be locked. Debating whether to force one he suddenly heard his pursuers again—on the back stairs, and storming up them. It was too late for escape. Jaw gone hard he set himself, reluctant but ready to use the gun if he had to.

And then a door across the way swung open; the man who stepped out saw him there and halted with one hand on the knob and the other holding what looked to be a leather cigar case. It was Frank Stroud.

For a moment, both stared. Stroud looked at the drawn gun, and then toward the corridor's far end and the sound of trampling feet in the stairwell. As quickly as that he appeared to size the situation up; without hesitation he opened the door wider, gesturing. Bannister had no time to weigh a decision. Wordlessly he slipped through the opening. The door swung closed behind him and he whirled to face it, waiting with held breath.

Excited voices reached him, muffled by the panel. "Mr. Stroud, you seen a man go by here?"

By contrast, Stroud's reply was unruffled, coolly self-possessed. "Why, no. I haven't seen a soul. I just came up to my room to get some cigars. Of course, I *was* inside with the door shut, for a minute or two. What seems to be the trouble?" he added. "I thought I heard shooting . . ."

But they weren't wasting time answering questions. One muttered an impatient word or two, and they were gone, the sound of their boots quickly receding farther along the corridor. A moment later the door opened. Stroud entered and closed it after him; he put a key into the lock and turned it, tested the knob. That done, he turned and laid a quizzical look on Jim Bannister.

"Well," he said. "This would seem to square us for whatever happened at the church this evening, when Ridge Decker failed to do the job I pay him for."

Bannister nodded. "Yes, I guess it does." Still cautious, he lowered the gun he was holding but made no move to put it away. Stroud observed this. He calmly proceeded to take a cigar from the leather case. All the time maintaining a cool stare on Bannister's face, he bit off the end of the cigar and spat it out, fished up a match and snapped it into life on his thumbnail.

He said calmly, "So, suppose *you* tell me—just what the devil is going on around this hotel, that I'm not in on?"

The business in the manager's office hadn't gone quite as Arch Caverhill foresaw it, nor did it take much time. Frank Stroud appeared to know already the legal description of the Holbrook property. Not waiting for Elgin to explain anything, he simply took the draft of the transfer document from the lawyer's hand and glanced over it, had a brief look at the markings on the map, and—a little stiffly—declared himself satisfied.

Actually relations between Stroud and Caverhill had become strained lately, over the latter's refusal to sign the property transfer until Sunday's ceremony was over. There was no way this could be made to look like anything but lack of trust in the man his niece was marrying. Nevertheless he was standing stubbornly by his guns, and Stroud had had to go along whatever he thought of it. Once the ceremony was over and Stroud and Emily were man and wife, Arch would sign the deed; not a minute before.

So now Frank Stroud handed the lawyer back his papers, excused himself to go and fetch the cigar case he had forgotten upstairs in his room, and left. The whole business had taken no more than five minutes.

Alone with the lawyer, Arch Caverhill swore but, afterward, with a shrug, said roughly, "Well, you done what I asked; thanks anyway for your trouble. And maybe we bought some time, after all." He was talking more or less to himself; Elgin, who had no idea why he had been instructed to help get Stroud away from the supper table, could only look at him blankly. Caverhill added, "You have the fair copy all ready to sign, do you?"

"In my safe," the lawyer said. The other nodded, said a brusk goodnight and walked out, leaving him to puzzle over this business if he wanted to.

Caverhill was crossing the lobby when the two gunshots sounded, somewhere in the hotel and so closely blended they could not have come from the same gun. He hauled up, scarcely aware of the reaction around him. He could only stand frozen and immobilized by a sickening fear for Emily's safety, breaking free of this when a Broken Spur hand named Karns, who had been stationed on the veranda by Wes Niles, came bursting in.

Karns saw his employer and exclaimed, "Arch! What was that shooting? Do you suppose—?"

He didn't finish. At that moment Stew Gilson erupted out of the back hallway, ashen of face and carrying a smoking gun. A man of no great courage, he answered Caverhill's sharp question in a stammer. "Boss, hell's breakin' loose back there!" Caverhill waited for no more. He brushed past Gilson, with a look of iron. Followed by the pair from Broken Spur he hurried off to see what danger might have involved his niece.

He found her alone in the private dining room; she stood and stared at nothing as though in a state of shock, cheeks as white as the knuckles of the hand that gripped the back of a chair. A second chair lay overturned and drifts of acrid gunsmoke hung motionless over the table and the wreckage of the meal that had been eaten there. Alarmed by Emily's manner, Caverhill placed a hand on her shoulder as he demanded anxiously, "Girl! Are you all right?"

She managed a nod. But then he saw he had been followed and the hallway was clogged with people from the lobby, and even a late diner or two with napkins tucked forgotten into waistcoats. His temper slipped its bonds and he advanced on them, saying angrily, "Come on— come on, now! We don't need an audience. This is a private matter. Karns," he ordered his man, "get them away from here! And you, Gilson—see if you can find Wes Niles . . ."

There was no door, only a curtain to cover the opening. Metal rings sang on the rod as he pulled it to; when he turned back to his niece he remembered to keep his voice down, so his words would not carry. "You better have a seat," he said, with as much gentleness as he could muster. But she remained as she was, unmoved by his urging. He gave it up. "Can you tell me what happened? What's become of that Bonner sonofabitch?"

His niece spoke, in a dead voice, not answering the question. She said instead, "The whole thing was arranged, wasn't it? All of it—the lawyer, and the business with the papers. Just the other day, you told me the details about the deed had been taken care of. But you wanted Frank out of the room, so that man and I would be left alone . . ."

Caverhill's protest sounded lame in his own ears. "Whatever put such ideas in your head?"

"*He* did—Bonner! Something he said, when Wes broke in on us . . ." She turned to him. "Why do we go on pretending? You know about me—*everything* about me. You've known all along!"

"Girl, I got no idea what—" But the clumsy protest broke off under the weight of her look, and Arch Caverhill could only shake his head in angry despair. "Damn it, I was determined you wouldn't ever have to know I'd found out. . . ."

Emily's eyes had brimmed with tears; her mouth drew out long and began to tremble. She dropped her glance, unable to hold it. "But how can you bear," she said in a muffled voice, "to have anything at all to do with me, when—?"

He cut her off, speaking with deliberate intensity as he looked down on her lowered head. "Now, you listen! You're my only kin—and the nearest I'll ever come to having a daughter of my own. To me, *that's* what matters. As for anything in the past—well, I know what that brother of mine was! He was a scamp, who never had it in him to make proper provisions to take care of a family. Whatever you had to do, it was just a matter of staying alive; and it don't concern me.

"You begun a new life when you came to Broken Spur," he went on doggedly, "and I've tried to do all I can to make it a good one. Anything you got your heart set on, I mean for you to have. Ain't nothing on this earth," he said with emphasis that brought her head up slowly, "not a thing that's good enough for my girl. I want you to understand that—and I want you to know I mean it!"

Slowly she turned, showing him tear-wet cheeks that were stiff with disbelief. She was tall enough that there was not too great a disparity in their heights, as she stood before him studying the gaunt face whose fierceness was softened, just now, by emotion. "If you do mean this," she told him haltingly, "if you aren't ashamed to admit being kin to me—then I don't ask anything else!" And on impulse she kissed one of his leathery, wrinkled cheeks.

Awkwardly the old man slipped an arm about her shoulders. "Sho' now!" he grunted. "Everything's going to be all right. I'm just sorry as hell I made you talk to that Bonner! But, it was the only way I could think of to find out, as quick as possible, just what he had in mind and what he knew. Well, I guess we found out!"

"He knows everything," she said miserably. "He's even had the Pinkertons after me!"

Arch Caverhill swore at that. "All right," he

said fiercely. "It won't do him a bit of good—that's a promise!"

Abruptly then he turned away, and yanked the curtain aside. Seeing no one in the hall he told his niece, "You best go on up to your room and wait there, while I find out what's happening. And don't worry about Bonner. Even if I have to kill him myself, he ain't going to have the chance to hurt you!"

Chapter VII

Having delivered Emily to her room, with a suggestion that its door be kept locked as a precaution, Arch Caverhill descended the lobby stairs. He found that excitement over the shooting had mostly ended; he read veiled interest in the eyes that turned toward him but he ignored them all. Stew Gilson was standing near the street door and Caverhill went directly to him to ask gruffly, "Any news?" Getting a glum headshake he added, "Where's Niles? You see him?"

"Just stepped outside . . ."

On the dark veranda, the oil lamps bracketing the door failed to show any sign of his foreman. Dunbar's main street lay obscurely in the star glow, its single row of lighted buildings facing the river channel. After a moment Wes Niles came around the corner of the building; he saw his boss standing by the veranda rail and came up to join him. "Where the hell you been?" Caverhill demanded testily.

"Hunting Bonner. Looks like he got away."

"Got *away!* A second time? How the hell could that be?"

"My fault, Arch," Niles admitted. "He's slippery—as I had good reason to know, after what he done to me at the ranch. This time I swear

I tried to think of everything. I had our boys stationed at every outside door; trouble is, they didn't stay put. Minute they heard the shooting, they all went busting in to take a hand. Looks like that only made it possible for the sonofabitch to slip past them. My fault," he said again. "I ought to make sure they'd follow orders."

"Don't blame yourself," Caverhill said gruffly. "You can't think of everything . . . But tell me," he added, "just what *did* go on in that dining room? Even after getting Emily's version, I'm still in the dark."

"She's all right, is she?" Wes Niles asked quickly, and was clearly relieved to get an affirmative answer. Caverhill listened, then, to an account of the talk Niles had overheard before finally deciding the stranger had revealed enough, harried Emily enough, and that the time had come to put an end to it. "The bastard! I should have had him cold—but damned if he didn't turn the tables on me a second time! By God, if I ever get another chance—!"

"All right, Wes," Caverhill said, to tone him down. "Let's hear the rest. Stew Gilson tried to step in—?"

"Yeah, and got driven off. And while I was hunting my gun, Bonner headed for the back hall. I don't know how our boys could have missed him but somehow they never seen hide nor hair. So I been out looking around, myself. He's gone!"

Arch Caverhill was scowling fiercely into the darkness, pulling with thumb and forefinger at his saber of a nose. "I doubt he'd go far. No blackmailer gives up that easy, not one with half the gall of this Bonner—or whatever his name really is. No, you can count on it; he'll be back."

"How can you tell? Maybe his next move will be to take and sell what he knows to Frank Stroud, for whatever he can get."

Caverhill shook his head. "He'd be too smart for that. Once he talks, that's it—he's used up his ammunition. He'll figure there's a lot more profit in it if he can just find a way to bleed me dry."

"Can he do that?" Niles demanded bluntly, peering at the dimly seen features of his boss. "You gonna pay, Arch?"

"Like hell I'm gonna pay!" the older man snorted. "It's the worst thing you can do with his kind—once you start, there's never an end!" He shook his head stubbornly. "I tell you now, this is gonna be the sorriest blackmailer that ever got too big for his boots!" As another thought struck him he demanded, "What about Gilson? How much did he overhear?"

"None at all," Niles quickly assured his boss. "I was damned careful about that. I kept him out of earshot till I seen I was in trouble."

"That's good."

They were silent a moment, while the sound of the river, amplified against the opposite canyon wall, reached to them and the pine trees around the hotel rocked against the stars. Wes Niles, a restless man, asked presently, "What do I do now?"

The older man stirred himself, his decision already made. "I want you to have one of our boys hitch up the rig that's in the hotel stable, and bring it around. I'm taking Emily back to the ranch."

"Tonight? But everybody knows your plan was to stay in town till after the doings on Sunday."

"The hell with what everybody knows! I guess I can change my mind, can't I? The thing is, if this Bonner figures on further dealings with me I want it to be at Broken Spur, where I'll have the advantage—not here, under the eyes of the whole town!"

The other nodded slowly. "Yeah, I see that, Arch. But ain't the real damage already done? A town this size, anybody that ain't already heard about this business tonight is soon going to be wondering a lot. And that includes the marshal. Blackman's a good enough law officer but he's a nosy one. What will you tell *him?*"

"That it's none of his damn business," Caverhill snapped. "Because, by God, it ain't!"

"Well, maybe . . . But that won't go down with Frank Stroud," the foreman reminded him. "Not if he finds out Emily was involved. And he'll have a right. After all, come Sunday—"

"It ain't Sunday yet! You let me worry about

handling Frank Stroud. He's getting himself a pretty good deal, with this marriage. Until that deed is legally signed, he'll do himself a favor to watch his step with me and not give me any problems. But hell—we're wasting time," Caverhill added, interrupting himself sharply. "Will you go have that rig brought up, like I ordered you?"

"Sure." But Niles still held back. He blurted suddenly, "Just one other thing, Arch: What about Emily? Could you tell how she's taking this? To have the past thrown in her face like that, without warning—it must have been damned rough on her!"

"She's taking it fine," Caverhill assured him. Then, frowning, he added, "One thing I guess I better tell you, though: I'm afraid we didn't put anything over on her, this evening. That business with the lawyer and the deed—it wasn't as clever as I thought. She asked me flat out, and I couldn't lie and make it stick. I had to own up."

Niles' face fell. "Oh, hell, Arch! I'm sorry! That was the last thing you and I ever wanted—that she should know you'd found out. It must have been humiliating for you both."

Arch Caverhill admitted it with a heavy nod. "Well, it's done—and after all these months I guess it's sort of cleared the air. At least I no longer have to watch my step with her. All I have to do now, is try to convince her this makes no difference between us . . ."

Plainly distressed, Wes Niles would have answered something but at that moment they were interrupted, as three men turned off the plank sidewalk and came up the steps of the hotel veranda. The trio consisted of Harry Lantry, and Sam Reeves in his horsehide vest, and another small rancher named Jess Pryor. They had seen the pair in the dim glow of the oil lamp and Lantry called uncertainly, "Arch? Is that you?" And when he got an affirmative grunt in answer: "We'd like to talk to you."

Caverhill hesitated, but said, "All right. Just a minute . . ." Turning back to his foreman he said, "You know what you're to do. While you're at it, you better go up to Emily's room and tell her the change in plans. Lend her a hand if she needs it, getting ready to leave."

Wes Niles nodded and went off about his duties. With some reluctance, then, Arch Caverhill turned to face his neighbors as they confronted him there on the dark veranda.

"Well?"

They seemed uneasy but grimly determined. Harry Lantry, who appeared to be the spokesman, cleared his throat. "First off: What Tobe Munkers done, earlier this evening—whether you believe it or not, I'm telling you again, we never put him up to that. It was the whiskey he'd been drinking, nothing else. Had we realized the condition he was in, we'd have kept closer tabs on him.

114

That's God's truth! But, he caught us flat footed!"

Caverhill considered that, recognizing the sincerity in the words and seeing it reflected in the anxious faces of Lantry's friends. He nodded. "All right. Knowing Munkers, I have to believe you. It isn't the kind of behavior I'd expect from you people," he admitted. "I see no call to hold the rest of you responsible."

"That's good to hear you say," Lantry told him.

"Then if it's settled—"

"Actually, that ain't why we came." Harry Lantry drew a breath. "Arch, we three are taking it on ourselves to speak for all of us that depend on the Holbrook Lease for our summer range. I know it's a little late in the day to be offering deals, but—well, we been making medicine over this thing. And we were wondering . . ."

He hesitated and Caverhill prodded him, not liking this and coldly determined to have it over. "Yes?"

"Arch, what will you take for that property? Name a price, and somehow or other—we'll try to meet it."

As Arch Caverhill stared, taken aback, Sam Reeves spoke up. "We're dead serious! There's just no way any of us can do without our summer range—lose it, and we may as well throw in our hands. But, damn it, we can't do that! We've all worked too long, and too hard, on those spreads of ours!"

"Name your own price," Lantry repeated. "If it's anything in reason, we won't fuss or try to cut it down. What's more, we'll pay cash—even if it means putting our outfits under mortgage!"

Scowling fiercely, the Broken Spur rancher looked from one to another of the trio facing him. "You honest to God mean this?"

"We speak for ourselves," Lantry said, "but I guarantee the rest will go along. Even Tobe Munkers—and what's more, we'll pledge surety for his behaving himself in future. We'll make that part of the deal. Like Sam says, we're dead serious!"

More troubled than he liked to admit, Caverhill found himself growing a little angry at the pressure. To end this before it went any further, he broke in now as Jess Pryor started to speak. "Sorry, but I'm afraid you've wasted your time. The property you're talking about is already disposed of."

"But that ain't so!" Sam Reeves protested. "Everybody knows the papers ain't actually been signed yet."

"It's all the same. I've given my promise." Why did they have to stand there looking at him like that, as though their world had crumbled about their ears—and Arch Caverhill could somehow prevent it?

It was Harry Lantry who answered him, in a voice that had lost its fire. "We've been neigh-

116

bors a long time, Arch," he said slowly. "I even sort of thought we could call you a friend. But maybe being a friend—or even a neighbor—don't signify any longer . . ."

"Oh, hell!" Sam Reeves spoke out of bitter emotion. "We all know it's just part of the price to buy his niece a husband!"

A burst of hot anger leaped in Arch Caverhill, consuming any compassion he might have been fighting against. "I'll thank you to leave my Emily out of this!"

"How can we?" Reeves retorted. "When she's the real reason—"

Lantry cut him off. "Let it go, Sam," he said in a leaden tone. "You'll only make matters worse. You can see it isn't going to change his mind."

"Then maybe," Reeves shot back, "it's up to us to think of something that will!"

Arch Caverhill stiffened, hearing that. "Oh? Are you maybe threatening me?"

Harry Lantry moved quickly. His shoulder took Reeves in the chest, fairly staggering him. "Let's be going," Lantry growled, got the other two turned away and then, without allowing for argument, simply shooed them toward the veranda steps. There he paused, long enough to look back over a shoulder; his seamed and weathered face was deeply troubled as he said, "Arch, I'm sorry. I was hoping—" He gave it up, cut himself off with a shrug. Next moment the three men had

117

dropped down the steps and turned away along the sidewalk, and the ragged tramp of their boots on sun-warped planks came back after they had vanished.

They left Arch Caverhill aware all at once of the cold strike of the night wind against his face, that was flushed with the heat of anger; he found himself clenching his fists till the nails dug into the palms. That those men would have the gall! The insinuation that he had to buy a husband for his niece—the half-veiled warning that they would find some way to make him cancel his promised plans for the Holbrook property—it was enough to strike a proud man to the quick and stiffen his resolve.

His indignation, at that moment, was nearly enough to blot out the gnawing of an uneasy feeling of guilt. . . .

Someone went bustling through the corridor outside Frank Stroud's room. He cocked his head at the sound, and looked at Jim Bannister through a screen of smoke from his cigar. "They haven't given up," he said wryly.

Jim Bannister sat in a straight chair, near a window where he could look down into the side street below while its curtain gave him some protection from being seen. He said, "I can wait a few minutes longer."

Stroud blew a perfect smoke ring at the lamp,

and looked at the glowing end of the cigar to make sure it was burning evenly. "And you're determined you aren't going to tell me what's been going on here?"

"Oh, I might," Bannister told him coolly, "if I thought it was any of your business. But it happens to concern me and Arch Caverhill."

"*And* his niece," Stroud pointed out. "The woman I'm pledged to marry . . . I'm not completely dense, Bonner," he went on, his eyes pinning the man seated by the window. "A fool could have seen that that business with the lawyer was all staged—a trick, no less, to get me out of the way so the two of you would be alone, for whatever reason. I have a right to know what happened between you and her, that's all at once sent Broken Spur gunning for you."

"I'd suggest you ask Miss Caverhill."

"I'm asking you!" the other snapped. "And while I'm at it, there's another thing that wasn't any accident: you just happening to be waiting across the street from the church, where you could step out and make your play with that crazy bastard, Munkers." Stroud shook his head, his eyes stony. "You take all this, along with some other unanswered questions I have about those Caverhills—it adds up to something very damned peculiar!"

Bannister said, "You're making long guesses. I'll say it again: None of it has anything to do with you. You'll simply have to take my word."

"Your word!" Stroud repeated heavily. He made a curt slicing gesture with the cigar, that drew a line of blue-black smoke in the still air of the room. "What good is that to me?"

Jim Bannister managed to quell a stir of anger. "None, I suppose," he answered sharply. "If you don't even trust the woman you're marrying on Sunday!"

He saw Frank Stroud stiffen as though a poker had been rammed up the middle of his back; the black eyes pinned Bannister with a physical force. Returning the look, he was coldly determined that whatever the other wanted from him he wasn't going to get it. Despite Emily Caverhill's refusal to help him, he would not betray her secret to this man she had chosen to marry; that would be too petty a revenge. If Frank Stroud had his suspicions, he thought bleakly, let him hire the Pinkertons and dig out the sordid facts for himself! He owed Stroud nothing. Each had done the other a favor this evening; the slate was clean.

Just now Stroud's sallow cheeks were darkened with angry color. He opened his mouth and closed it again—for once, at least, at a loss for words. What he might have answered went unspoken, then, for without warning there came an abrupt and guarded rapping at the door.

At once Bannister stiffened and touched the gun under his coat, but Frank Stroud gave him a brief shake of the head. "Decker," he said, and went to turn the key in the lock and swing the door open.

Ridge Decker sidled in, giving the impression that he always moved carefully going through doorways. On closer view Stroud's bodyguard was not too impressive—a little less than average height, sallow-skinned, with a heavy jaw and curious muddy eyes. He wore the tail of his coat pulled back, revealing the basketweave holster and wooden-handled revolver—almost like a badge of office. He hauled up short, as he saw the man seated by the window.

"Him! I'll be damned! They been tearing the building apart, hunting this sonofabitch. Don't tell me he's been here all the time?"

"Most of it," Stroud said as he closed and locked the door again. Bannister returned the gunman's stare, with a certain wariness in both of them as they sized each other up. Decker's employer asked him now, "What have you been hearing?"

"About five hundred different rumors," Decker said, and the corners of his mouth lifted in a wicked grin as he added, "From the talk, most seem to think he was caught trying to rape the Caverhill woman."

"Nonsense!" Bannister snapped, and looked sharply at the rancher. "Do I look that big a fool?" The black eyes rested on him and for a brief instant they seemed to burn with suspicion.

But Bannister met the look squarely and after a moment Stroud turned back to his gunman.

Not pursuing that question he asked, "Are they still hunting for him?"

"I kind of think they've given up. At least they seemed satisfied he can't be in the hotel. But I also understand the old man's changed his plans about staying in town tonight. One of his hands has already gone to fetch his rig from the stable, out back."

"Oh?" At that moment there was the sound of a team and vehicle moving through the side street below the open window. Slanting a look down, without exposing himself, Jim Bannister saw a fancy-looking surrey being driven around to the front of the hotel, apparently having just been taken from the stable at the rear.

A shadow fell upon him and he turned his head to find Stroud looking past his shoulder. The man gave a grunt of surprise. "It looks," he said to Ridge Decker, "as though you're right. That's certainly Caverhill's rig."

Stroud turned from the window, frowning; he seemed suddenly to reach a decision, then started for the door as though he meant to learn for himself what Caverhill was up to. At that, Bannister came quickly to his feet, only to see Ridge Decker drop a hand to the gun in his basketweave holster.

"And where do you think *you're* going?"

Bannister halted, looked coldly at the gunman and then at Stroud who had paused with a hand on the doorknob. Impatient and determined not to give any ground to a hired gun like Decker, he said, "Call him off!"

The man's head jerked around for a questioning glance at his employer, and received the briefest of nods. His muddy eyes squinted. "But I thought—"

"He's not a prisoner," Stroud said. "Let him go. I'll explain later."

Decker showed his puzzlement but he gave no argument, though the look he gave Bannister was black with dislike, and with all the feisty resentment of a small man for a big one. And watching these two together—seeing the firm control Frank Stroud maintained over someone as dangerous as the gunman—crystallized a question that Jim Bannister realized had been nagging at him, all along.

Just how well did Emily Caverhill think she knew the person she was marrying? Unless Stroud had somehow managed to hide his true nature from her, it was a mystery to Bannister what she could find to want in this cold-eyed, and to him completely repellant, man. But maybe the answer lay in her own shadowy past: Abandoned by her lovers, driven to the streets, it was conceivable the one thing she hungered for above all else, now, was simply respectability.

And if Frank Stroud appealed to her as someone successful and ambitious and solidly rooted, marriage to him might seem a way of wiping out the stain of the lost years.

On the other hand, perhaps this was actually something her uncle wanted: it might even be that, against her own feelings, she saw it as the only way of repaying the debt she owed Arch Caverhill for virtually rescuing her from the gutter. In either case she was making a bargain she might live to regret; still, she was a mature woman and her life was her own, and presumably she knew what she wanted to do with it.

Bannister meanwhile had his own concerns. He had spent an uncomfortably long time in this room. If Ridge Decker was right and the hunt for him had settled down, it was as good a moment as any to clear out. Ignoring Decker's suspicious scowl, he started for the door.

Stroud said quickly, "Let me check first." He worked the key and glanced into the hall, and with a nod opened the door wide. "Seems clear enough."

"Thanks."

Bannister stepped through, had his look in both directions along the double line of closed doors. After that he was heading, at a soundless prowl, toward the rear stairway. He could all but feel Frank Stroud's cold stare following him until he was out of sight.

Chapter VIII

For some minutes after Niles entered her room, neither he nor Emily Caverhill spoke. She had turned away, leaving it for him to close the door; in real concern he looked at the dispirited droop of her shoulders as she stood by the bed, one hand resting on the brass frame, her gaze on the black square of the window. After a moment he went to the dresser, where he found a couple of tumblers. He had brought a bottle in a pocket of his coat. He poured out a couple of fingers into each tumbler, filled hers the rest of the way with water. He carried it over to her, watched her take the drink and finish it off, without a word, and make a face over it. He tossed his own off neat, and returned both glasses where he found them.

"Does that help a little?" he suggested, with a gentleness that might have surprised anyone who knew the tough and efficient ramrod of Broken Spur.

When the woman made no answer he plunged ahead with what he had come to tell her, driven as usual with the many pressures put on him by his job. "That Bonner fellow got away from us, after all. My fault, I guess—I tried to think of everything but I missed somewhere. And so, you had to go and be put through all that, for nothing!"

She still didn't look at him. "It doesn't matter," she said, with the smallest of shrugs.

"The hell it doesn't! It must have come as the shock of your life, not having the slightest hint of what was coming—to be left alone with him like that, and have him suddenly open up on you! It wasn't no way fair; but under the circumstances—All we knew about him for certain, was that he'd been to the ranch asking for you, but never a hint of what he wanted. There didn't seem any other way to make him show his hand—"

He broke off as she turned to him and, for the first time, he became aware of the stricken look in her eyes. Niles had come to admire her strength in surviving the bad years before she came to Broken Spur; but there was a beaten and injured quality in her now that shocked him into exclaiming, "Emily! What is it?"

"*You* told him," she accused, in a leaden tone. "*You* told him about me!"

"But I never! I swear! Why in the world should I do that—with some total stranger?"

She shook her head impatiently. "No, no. Not Bonner. I mean *him*—my uncle! Everything you've heard from me, in confidence—tonight he admitted he knows the whole story! You just passed it along," she went on while he stared at her, unable to speak, "though you knew the

126

one thing I dreaded, after all he's done for me, was that he should have to learn the truth! If I hadn't been afraid all the time something would happen—just like what did happen today—and make a situation I couldn't handle alone, I never would have confided in you. You were someone I thought I could trust. And instead—"

She could say nothing more. The speech died in her throat, and she let a hopeless gesture of one hand complete it for her. Wes Niles stood silent a moment, aghast—only beginning to understand how the life she had managed to make for herself here must appear to be falling apart.

He found his tongue. "Yeah, I can see it's got to look like I betrayed you. But will you listen?" When she neither moved nor spoke, he drew a long breath, and plunged ahead. "You mustn't forget, your uncle is a pretty important man in this State, worth a lot of money. When he first heard from you, naturally he had to be careful—take steps to make sure you were really who you said, and not somebody out to bilk him. Of course, soon as he got to know you he told me he never had another doubt. But he'd already had investigations started, and after a while they began getting results."

Emily had lifted her head and turned to Niles; her face was colorless. "I see . . ."

"I guess what he heard was mostly true, but it wasn't the whole story. Nothing at all about that bastard Wells McGraw, and what he done to you. The reports got Arch terrible upset, because he was already starting to feel like you was the daughter he never had. So—" He hesitated. "So I told him everything, because it was better he know the whole story and not just half!

"Emily, he understood! And when he did, the only thing he cared about was that you shouldn't know your secret wasn't a secret any longer. He wanted nothing changed, wanted everything to go on just as it had before. Of course, it took pretending and it put me square in the middle, but that was all right. We just didn't either of us want to see you hurt, ever again."

Emily Caverhill's hand, clasping the brass frame of the bedstead, was so tight that the knuckles showed white through the skin. After a long moment she said, in a dull tone, "I suppose, if you have to choose between being despised and being pitied—"

"Now, get that out of your head!" Wes Niles exclaimed. "Arch *loves* you. He ain't much practiced at showing it, but I know him well—and it's true!

"Right now," he went on gruffly, because time was passing and he hoped to break her out of this mood, "we got a blackmailer on our hands, who's got to be stopped from doing anything to ruin your wedding. Arch don't think he'll go to Stroud—not yet, before he's had one more crack at getting money out of the Caverhills; and if he tries that, we want it to be at Broken Spur, not here in town. So I been sent to tell you to get your stuff together. We're leaving for the ranch, almost immediately."

She accepted this without argument, even though it was clear she understood she was being used to set a trap. She placed a carpetbag on the bed and then went to the clothes press and began taking out the dresses and other things she had carefully hung there, only a few hours before. Watching, Wes Niles tried to read the thought behind her expressionless mask. Above all he wished he could know if she had decided to forgive him for betraying a confidence. He simply hadn't the nerve to ask.

All at once the urge for another shot from the bottle on the dresser was terribly strong, but he resolutely vetoed it.

In the corridor outside he heard a door open, and hurried bootsteps moved quickly along the hallway; for some reason this reminded him again of the man named Bonner, and he told Emily with as much assurance as he could manage, "You're not to fret about that blackmailer, you hear? Our crew's been alerted. Naturally they ain't been told any more than they absolutely need to know. They're good ol' boys, they'll follow orders; and if they figure it's none of their business they won't ask any questions as to what it might be all about. They've got his description and the description of his horse. They're hunting the town for him this very minute.

"If he has the gall to show himself again—here, or at Broken Spur—believe me, we'll be ready for him!"

The darkness was full of movement and small noises; tree branches and thick brush stirred, rocked by the wind that breathed along the canyon and pushed at Bannister as he ghosted his way toward the spot where he had tethered the dun. Men were abroad in the night, as well. Only minutes earlier he had knelt in the dark slot between the hotel and an adjoining building and watched as the Broken Spur crew set out, Arch Caverhill hurrying his niece down the veranda steps and into the waiting surrey, and climbing in beside her. There had been a restless mill of horsemen. As Caverhill touched up his team and sent his rig rolling north along the street, starting the trip back to the ranch, a half dozen of the crew fell in behind like an armed escort.

Wes Niles and four riders remained. More than a little puzzled, Bannister had watched them, hearing the run of Niles' deep voice without being able to make out what instructions were being given. Abruptly the four riders had swung their bridles and jingled away in a group, south out of Dunbar along the canyon road; Niles saw them off, then pulled his own horse around and spurred in the wake of the vanishing surrey. Bannister was left frowning in puzzlement, as the dry and acrid dust, stirred by all this activity, settled and was dispersed on the night wind.

He was still wondering now about those four riders, and why they should have sent them off down canyon in a direction opposite from Broken Spur. He moved with caution, gun in hand, keeping to the shadows because he didn't believe for a minute all of Caverhill's men had left town—there were sure to be others, still searching. A moon had risen above the canyon walls, and these swaying trees put down a confusing pattern of shifting light and shadow. Despite an outdoorsman's trained sense of direction, he was beginning to wonder if he had lost his bearings.

Then the trees fell away and there, in a narrow clearing not five yards in front of him, his horse stood waiting just where he had tied it. The windy busyness of the night had the dun uneasy. It was stirring around, pulling at its tether and making unhappy snorting sounds, and Bannister was about to move forward and try to reassure and settle it when all of a sudden he froze, aware that someone was approaching.

Whoever it was must be closing in on the commotion the spooked animal created. Dry branches crackled as they were brushed aside. Now a man stepped into the open—only a vague shape, in that confusion of shadows, but near enough that Bannister heard the startled intake of breath at his discovery. For a moment the man held where he was; after that he was starting for the dun, reaching to take the reins that held it anchored.

Bannister said sharply, "Don't touch that horse!"

The surprise he caused was total. It brought the other man wheeling around so abruptly his boots nearly tangled in the underbrush. But he caught himself and in the next breath he started a convulsive movement. Bannister rightly guessed he was trying for a gun.

Jim Bannister could have shot him, but instead he lunged forward, trying to reach him before he could get his weapon out of leather. But the dun, already frightened, was startled by the sudden movement; it pulled back on the reins, snorting in terror, and swung around directly in Bannister's path so that he barely managed to avoid colliding with the heavily muscled haunch. A hoof lashed out, the steel shoe grazing his shin—it would have smashed the leg had it struck squarely. As it was Bannister stumbled and went to one knee. And then the horse, still fighting its reins, swept wildly around in the other direction and the way was cleared, giving him a glimpse of moonlight on the barrel of that other revolver. That spurred him to his feet, and in two more strides he closed the distance.

His opponent was a beanpole of a man, only slightly shorter than Bannister but lacking his weight—he was sure it was one of the Broken Spur crew that he had seen pouring into the back hallway of the hotel after the dining room confrontation with Wes Niles and the one called Gilson. Barreling into him, Bannister carried the man backward until the bole of a tree stopped them. Groping, he found the hand that contained the gun and he clamped down on it, trying to twist and make it release the weapon. The other was wiry, though, and he was tough. Using the tree trunk at his back to brace him he brought up his head suddenly, and the top of the hard skull caught Bannister solidly on the jaw.

As his head snapped back, the hat sailing from it, he felt his teeth click together and spots of colored light swept across his vision. Briefly stunned, he lost his hold and the hand with the gun was jerked free of his numbed fingers. But he still had his own revolver and, with no chance to aim a blow, he swung it. The long barrel struck the tree trunk with a force that nearly jarred the weapon from his fingers; but the figure he was struggling with went suddenly limp and became a dead weight. Still dazed himself, Bannister felt it slide out of his grasp. He could only step back and let the man drop to the ground at the foot of the tree.

With his own head clearing, he knelt and examined the limp form of the Broken Spur man. There was a steady pulse; then exploring fingers located a warmth of blood on the man's left cheekbone, and he knew that blow with the gunbarrel hadn't entirely missed. The man had been hit hard enough to stun him and lay him out cold, for the moment.

Bannister wiped his fingers dry on pine needle litter as he knelt there, testing the stillness. If anyone else was searching this area, it would appear they hadn't heard the scuffle. Just the same, he knew now that he should waste no more time getting out of Dunbar; the town was too hot for him, and there was nothing more he could hope to do here. He hunted around for the hat he had lost, and also found the gun dropped by his unconscious opponent—he tossed that off into the bushes. Afterwards he turned to the dun.

Hearing Bannister's voice reassured the animal, and it nudged his shoulder as he took down his shell belt from the saddlehorn where he had left it. After replacing the spent load he holstered the revolver; he checked the cinch, freed his reins from the knot that anchored them and stood a moment, angrily considering.

It wasn't easy to admit failure, after having ridden so far—especially, having come within reach of the woman he'd hoped might answer some of his questions about the man he stood convicted of murdering. But with Broken Spur hunting him the odds for a second chance at Emily Caverhill looked fairly slim, even if there was still any possibility he could get her to talk. He recognized that he was up against a woman's stubbornness: She had lied to him, and once committed to a lie it just was not in a woman's nature to confess to it and change her story.

Nor could he blame her, really. He had to admire the courage of a woman trying to overcome the poor hand fate had dealt her; there'd been no pleasure in putting the screws to her, seeing the distress he caused with mention of Houston and Wells McGraw. He didn't know if he would want to go through that again—especially when he could see very little purpose in it.

Coming here in the first place had been a gamble and a long shot that had not paid off. Plainly the only sensible thing was to call it quits, and cut his losses. . . .

Then he thought of something that made him swear aloud, into the windy dark.

All of a sudden he knew why those four Broken Spur riders had been dispatched down the canyon—obviously they were an insurance policy against his doing just what he now had in mind, in trying to leave this place. They would be under orders from Wes Niles to stop him. They'd had time by now to set a trap at some convenient point, waiting and ready to spring whenever he happened to blunder into it. The more Bannister thought about this, the surer he grew—and the angrier.

"So that's how you want to play!" he said, in a tone that made the dun switch its ears. Though he couldn't stay where he was, he was damned if he intended to oblige his enemies by walking into a trap. Apparently they thought they had him bagged, but it was a bag with two mouths to it. He would simply use the one he already knew—backtracking was inconvenient and time-wasting but better than riding, blind, in country he'd never seen by daylight.

Stretched out along the canyon, Dunbar looked like more of a town than it actually was. To avoid being spotted by any other Broken Spur men who might have been left to keep the hunt going, he stayed off the main street and in back alleys where there were only scattered houses, and few lights showed. Presently the buildings thinned out to nothing; he glimpsed the bulk of the big livery barn, perched near the river channel, and a moment later came out at the northern end of the village. A faint glow of lamplight hung above the place. The river made a noisy accompaniment to the stillness. A nighthawk swooped startlingly past him, on silent wings.

Satisfied that no one had followed him,

Bannister spoke to the dun and sent it on up the canyon, retracing the route that had brought him down to Dunbar almost a dozen hours ago. To be doubling back like this was certainly far from what he'd planned; still, for the moment it was enough to be free of a town where he'd nearly met disaster.

Not that he was in the clear, yet. Far from it!

This wagon track, hugging a narrow shelf above the stretch of tumbling river, was after all the road to Broken Spur. When Arch Caverhill put his niece in a carriage and started for there it was very much as though he'd been deliberately setting bait—as though he were openly daring Bannister to come to the ranch for a second try at reaching her. And if, as he believed, Caverhill or Wes Niles had been sly enough to mount one trap for him in the lower canyon, he could hardly doubt there would be another waiting somewhere along here in case he did take the challenge.

So he rode cautiously, aware of the risk he could be running. There was no immediate sign of it; even the dust raised by the earlier passage of carriage and riders had had time to settle or be dissipated by the night wind. Anyone would have said he was utterly alone, with the brawling of the river at his right hand, and the lightly timbered walls that were alternately shadowed or touched with moonglow, according to the twists and turns the canyon made. But

Jim Bannister had learned to trust his instincts.

An hour deeper into the night, for all his caution he could still see no hint of trouble waiting.

He was getting close to the head of the canyon where, as he recalled, the river channel gentled out; if there was to be an ambush it would have to be somewhere very soon. In fact, he thought he knew the most likely place. Just ahead of him he could see how the canyon curved sharply around a blocky shelf of rock—an out-thrust of the mountain's flank. Beyond this he remembered a jumble of boulders, some nearly as large as a small house, that had fallen to block and change the river's course. Those boulders flanked the wagon road and made an ideal spot to lie in wait for an unsuspecting victim. Bannister had no intention of riding into it.

He had pulled in to sit listening to the busy activity of the river, and the fluting moan of the night wind in crevices of the rock. He was studying the formation to his left—like a giant knee thrust into the canyon, rising to a bench that was dotted with tall pines that clung to the rock; above this the flank of the mountain swept away less steeply. He recalled glimpsing a trail, earlier—nothing more than a horse track, nevertheless it would be a more direct route for riders coming down off the mountain on their way to town. He booted the dun ahead, now, riding slowly as he searched for it.

If he hadn't known what he was looking for he would likely never have spotted it, deceptively masked as it was by brush and tree shadow. He was already past when something made him glance back and then he saw it, as plain as anything. The trail proved steep to climb but no problem for a good horse like the dun. It snaked its way up through scattered trees and then, with one sharp switchback, gained the level of the bench; from there, he could see, it made easier grade along the mountain's flank, soon disappearing into timber. But first, he was interested in those boulders that would now be directly below him.

The canyon lay in deep shadow—black void from which rose the chill breath and sound of the unseen river. He reined as close as he dared for a look but could see nothing at all, and when the dun shifted its hoofs uneasily and dislodged a stone, the sound as it went clattering away was completely swallowed up in the racket of water pouring through its channel. Bannister spoke to calm the horse; he was about to pull back from the drop-off when a sudden spot of light flared briefly down there.

It vanished, but it left Bannister with a tight smile at the corners of his mouth as his guesses were confirmed. What he had seen was a match-flame, cupped between someone's palms as it was put to a cigarette. Probably the men

Caverhill stationed down there were growing tired of waiting; but if they meant to stay until the man they wanted came unsuspectingly along the canyon road, they had a long wait ahead of them.

The canyon road was closed to him, but the horse trail he was on now should take him across the flank of the mountain and eventually over the pass, quitting this country by the same route he entered it—had it really only been this morning? Well, he thought, he had taken a long ride and risked his neck, and apparently got nothing for it. But he had to consider his luck hadn't entirely deserted him. After all, he had found himself in a tight place or two here, but he had got out of them again. He supposed he had lost nothing, actually, except some time. . . .

Starting to climb once more, he found himself in moonlight that made the band of dark timber that hung above him look all the blacker. Though the swell of the mountain's flank should keep him out of sight of those Broken Spur men lying in wait below, he breathed easier to have the pines close around him at last.

As they did, there was a movement on his right. It caught at the edge of his vision and jerked his head around, while a hand started toward the butt of his gun. Behind him a voice said crisply, "Don't do it! Put both hands up by your ears, till we get a good look at you. . . ."

Chapter IX

Jim Bannister knew at once into whose hands he had fallen. Even before the man came walking toward him, gun leveled, he had recognized Bart Williams—the puncher who rode for Harry Lantry. Now a second one closed in on his other side; this man was mounted and enough moonlight shook down through the pine branches to show that he wore Sam Reeves' horsehide vest. A second gunbarrel glinted. Bannister raised his arms, as Williams reached and got the dun by the bridle.

A match flared, its head popped under a hard thumbnail. The quick burst of flame showed him Sam Reeves' sallow features and pale-lashed eyes, as he peered at the prisoner. When he shook out the match and tossed it aside, there was still a smear of afterimage. "Bonner!" Reeves exclaimed. "Just what I figured. From the size, it couldn't have been anyone else."

Bannister heard himself saying, with heavy irony, "It looks as though I rode around one trap—and straight into another!"

"We don't set traps, mister," Bart Williams retorted. "That's Broken Spur's style!"

"Oh? So what do you call this?"

"A bonus," Reeves answered curtly. He went

on to explain: "Broken Spur was just ahead of us as we came along the canyon, not a half hour ago—we could smell their dust. The moon hadn't tipped over yet, and once we climbed up here we could see them plain, bunched in them boulders at the Narrows. They was obviously waiting for somebody; Harry Lantry asked Bart and me to hang back and try to find out more."

Williams pointed out, "From the way you talk, you seem to figure it's *you* they was laying for, Bonner."

Bonner was reluctant to admit anything. He answered merely, "It pays to be careful," then added, "Do you mind if I put these hands down?"

"Not quite so fast!" Bart Williams snapped. "Nobody's taking any chances with you— there's been too damn many peculiar goings-on since you showed up, today. First, there was the grandstand play you made, moving in on Tobe Munkers and maybe saving that Frank Stroud bastard's hide for him. It must have really made an impression on the Caverhills—we understand you even had dinner with them at the Dunbar House.

"Then, next we hear, you've shot it out with Wes Niles and all at once Arch Caverhill is tearing up the ground trying to hunt you down! What you got to say about that?"

Bannister replied, "A man's apt to hear almost anything."

"You saying we heard wrong?"

"I'm only saying, what happened between me and Arch Caverhill is our business. . . ."

"Sonofabitch!" Suddenly Sam Reeves was closing on him and he saw the gleam of a gun-barrel rising, thought certainly it would descend and chop him out of the saddle. But Bart Williams spoke sharply and seemed to break through the other's anger; for the blow didn't land, though Reeves was breathing harshly as he lowered the gun.

Williams said to the prisoner, "It's no use asking, I suppose, what you happen to be doing here on the mountain at this time of night."

"I don't mind answering that, at least." Jim Bannister felt he owed the man something, for saving him from a likely pistol whipping. "I'm on my way out of this country. I finished my business in Dunbar and I was figuring to leave the way I came."

"Without even waiting for daylight?" Sam Reeves snorted in disbelief. "Hell! You're running from Broken Spur—try to deny it!"

Next moment Bannister felt his holster's weight go slack; Williams stepped back, holding the weapon he had lifted from the stranger's belt. He said flatly, "I think you better come with us."

Bannister looked at him. "Why should I? I have nothing to do with you people—even if, by accident, I do seem to keep running into you."

143

"This ought to be a good enough reason," the puncher replied shortly, and gestured with his gunbarrel. Bannister's jaw tightened.

"And where do you intend taking me?"

This time he got no answer at all. But Sam Reeves, still angry, offered him a heavy warning: "Don't give us no trouble. You can always travel face down, tied onto your saddle. It's your option."

There was no point in arguing; he held his tongue. Now Bart Williams vanished into the trees, returning a moment later with his horse. He mounted, and at his suggestion Reeves led out with the puncher bringing up the rear. Bannister supposed they were taking him to join Harry Lantry and the rest, but he wondered where. Not at one of the ranch headquarters, apparently, for this trail continued to take them higher on the mountain.

Time passed. The country grew more rugged and the night turned colder. Bannister, pulling his windbreaker closer about him, thought about those Broken Spur men back there in the canyon. It was a question at what point they would feel themselves justified to give up waiting for him, and go in and tell Arch Caverhill the trap he laid so carefully had come up empty. . . .

The moon had set, and despite their brilliance the glitter of the mountain star mesh wasn't the best light for traveling. Bannister had been in the saddle at dawn, and he was beginning to ask himself how long his captors meant to hold to this endless treadmill when, abruptly it ended. The single track merged with a clearly defined set of wagon ruts. They turned into this and followed it up an easy grade and into the gap of a couple of timbered ridges; and there below them, Jim Bannister saw the glow of lights.

Yellow squares were the lamplit windows of a house; starglow showed him, dimly, the shape of a barn and corral and other, smaller buildings. A tang of chimney smoke rode the night wind. This place looked too elaborate for an ordinary line camp, more likely a ranch headquarters; but it puzzled Bannister because he had understood that the outfits belonging to Lantry and Reeves and the rest of these men were all located in the valley. So, what place was this?

With the next breath he thought he knew, and the thought startled him. It could only be the Holbrook Lease headquarters!

The men he was riding with had pulled rein. Suddenly, in the darkness to their left, there was the unmistakable click of a rifle lever being worked. A voice with a tight edge to it challenged them: "Who's there? Declare yourselves!"

Reeves vented a startled grunt, but Williams called back, a shade impatiently, "That you, Sweeney? This is Bart—and Sam Reeves. Who did you *think* it was?"

The rider came toward them now, shaping up in the gloom as a figure in a battered range hat and bulky sheepskin coat, his rifle ready. From his voice he could be one of the men Bannister had seen at the roundup fire that morning. At the moment he sounded as though he were strung tight. "Only being careful," he said. "You could have been somebody from Broken Spur. I got orders to keep a close lookout, and—" He broke off, as he saw now they had a third horseman with them. "Hey! What the hell's this?"

"You might say it's a present for Harry."

"I don't get it!" Sweeney sounded perplexed. "Ain't he that Bonner gent?"

"Yeah—it's Bonner," Sam Reeves snapped, cutting in impatiently. "But right now we're waiting for news from *you*. What's the situation here? Did everything go according to plan?"

"Could have gone better," Sweeney admitted. "We were all of us hoping there wouldn't be any shooting."

"Shooting?" Bart Williams echoed sharply. "There ought not to been any at all. What went wrong?"

"I just ain't sure. Like we figured, Broken Spur only had a couple men posted here, and the seven of us took 'em by surprise. But afterwards, while I was out checking the barn, I'm told one of 'em got his hands on a gun someway and Lantry had to plug him. He ain't dead," Sweeney added, anticipating the question. "But I guess he's pretty bad hurt. They've done what they could for him. He's laying in the house there, now."

Williams demanded, "Anyone I know?"

"New man at Broken Spur, I understand. Somebody said his name is Honeycutt."

"Oh, hell! That's a shame!" Bart Williams said. "Joe Honeycutt struck me as a likely young fellow. Nearly signed on with us, when he first came here—only, Harry couldn't afford an extra hand so he went to Broken Spur. And now he has to get caught in the middle of a fracas that don't even concern him. It ain't right!"

Sam Reeves said gruffly, "Then why didn't he stay out of it? Fool should have known better than to try for a gun!"

Williams gave him a long look. "When a man works for *you,* Sam, I guess you expect him to back his iron!"

That sounded like an argument Reeves didn't feel much like pursuing. He passed it off by turning to Sweeney and demanding, "Any of our people get hurt?"

"Tobe Munkers took one in the arm. But I don't think it amounts to much."

Tobe Munkers, here? Bannister could hardly have been more surprised—the last he'd seen of the man was when he was being led off to jail by Marshal Blackman. He noticed that none of these colleagues seemed particularly disturbed over

147

the fact he'd been hurt. Sam Reeves commented, "Well, if that's all the damages I'd say we came off real good. I'm just sorry I had to miss the fun."

Sweeney hesitated. "I'm afraid I haven't told you quite all of it."

"How do you mean?" Williams demanded.

"Well—like I said, Caverhill had two men on the place. I'm afraid the other one got away."

"He did *what?*"

"I dunno how—but in the confusion he managed to slip out and grab off one of our horses. A couple of our boys took after him, but they ain't come back and it looks to me like he maybe gave them the slip!"

Bart Williams reacted as though he had been struck. "But, damn it! This blows the whole thing out of the water! Caverhill's gonna have warning and be on us before we can hope to get set for him!"

"That's why Clayt Jenkins and me been put on watch," Sweeney said, "against our being took by surprise. Lantry's sending out riders to fetch help from the other ranches, and to round up ammunition and extra guns. Though he still insists that Arch Caverhill would never actually use guns against his neighbors, if it was to come down to that."

Sam Reeves gave a snort. "Harry Lantry is a softheaded fool, to bet on it! By God, looks to me we better get down there and try to straighten him out!" He rammed the spurs, sending his horse jumping ahead. In the same breath he must have remembered the prisoner, for he cursed and swung back in a tight circle. His arm rose and fell, laying his rein-ends sharply across the rump of Bannister's dun. The animal's forward lunge nearly took Bannister by surprise, but he managed to catch his balance.

Under the spur and the sting of rein-ends, both horses struck at a pell-mell run toward the lamplit buildings that had been Tom Holbrook's ranch headquarters, with Bart Williams following close at their heels.

They didn't come unnoticed. As they stormed up before the house the door opened and someone stepped out, lamplight glinting on the rifle barrel in his hands. Bannister recognized Harry Lantry, as the latter called a challenge; Bart Williams sang out a reply, and then the horses were raising dust as they were jerked to a halt. On orders from one of his captors Jim Bannister dismounted, dropping his reins, and a moment later was being herded up the steps with Sam Reeves' gun prodding him. It was Reeves who said, "You see what we brung you, Harry."

Lantry was staring at the prisoner in stammering bewilderment. Bart Williams hurried to explain: "It's him that Broken Spur was laying for, there at the Narrows—only, we got him instead. It seems to me, if Arch Caverhill's really that anxious to lay hands on him he might be worth hanging on to. He could be useful, maybe, in a trade or a deal."

"That's a cold-blooded way to operate," Jim Bannister said bluntly. "You agree, Lantry?"

Lamplight showed the old man's troubled scowl. "I ain't sure I like it," he told the others. "Whatever trouble may have sprung up between this man and Arch Caverhill, he's done *us* no hurt; if anything, we ought to be glad he kept Tobe from blowing up a storm we couldn't handle, there at the church. In any event, it don't seem right to hand someone over to his enemies—to trade him off like he was a horse, or a steer!"

"Can we afford to be particular?" Sam Reeves demanded. "Before this night's over we may be glad for any kind of ace in the hole. I understand things here are in a damn bad way. . . ."

Harry Lantry lifted a hand and passed it over what was left of his thinning white hair. From over at the corral, a couple of horsemen went drumming suddenly out of the yard—on their way, Bannister supposed, to look for extra help or ammunition. Lantry dropped his arm. "All right," he said wearily. "Bring him on inside . . ."

A shove from Reeves propelled the prisoner across the threshold.

Anyone could have seen that this was no ordinary line shack, even if Broken Spur had in recent weeks been using it for one. Tom Holbrook had built it for his home, and he had built it sturdily—well aware, no doubt, of what a Colorado winter could be like in this sheltered cove on the mountain's flank. The log walls had been well chinked, and finished off on the inside. The main room, containing a wide stone fireplace, was furnished for cooking and eating, as well as to serve as living quarters for Holbrook and his wife; a bedroom, adjoining, had a curtain for a door.

Though Mrs. Holbrook must have added many homely touches, now that Broken Spur line riders had been batching here the man-sign was unmistakable. The place smelled of sweat and tobacco and bad cooking. A window pane had been carelessly punched out and stuffed with a wad of rags. A pair of chaps and a saddle rope decorated the peg where a picture had probably hung originally.

Tobe Munkers, a whiskey bottle and a tin cup in front of him, looked up as the men tramped in from outside. His left arm and shoulder were swathed in bandages and he appeared to be in pain; the whiskey he was drinking for it put a glitter in his eyes and a flush in his bony, beard-stubbled cheeks. His head jerked in surprise and clear dislike, as he saw Jim Bannister.

Bannister said to Harry Lantry, "I thought he was supposed to be in jail."

"That was only for his own protection," Lantry said, "until he sobered up. We promised the marshal we'd take care of him and see he kept out of trouble."

"Doesn't look that you've done too good a job. And if this is your way of sobering him up . . ."

Munkers only swore at him, hunched over his drink and gingerly nursed his gunshot arm. It was Sam Reeves who answered Bannister. "When we decided to take back the Lease, we knew we'd be needing every man we could get. Besides, we sure as hell weren't going to leave a hostage sitting in that jail, for Arch Caverhill to put his hands on!"

"It's none of my business," Bannister said, with a shake of the head. "But have any of you really thought about what you've done here? You've taken, by force, property belonging to another man. You've shot one of his punchers, who might even die. You've broken just about every law in the book. How can you hope to make this stick?"

"You're right, mister," Sam Reeves said harshly. "It *ain't* any of your business!"

But Harry Lantry acknowledged the seriousness of what Bannister had said, with a sober and troubled nod. "Bonner, you don't understand. We're desperate men. Maybe this will show Arch, once and for all, just *how* desperate—make him realize just what he's done to us. I'm sorry as hell about Joe Honeycutt; that was never intended. But we've gone too far now to turn back."

Bart Williams had gone immediately into the bedroom, to see just how it was with the wounded Broken Spur man. He came back now looking grim. "Joe needs a doctor, bad."

"Maybe you think *I* don't?" Tobe Munkers complained. "This damned arm's killing me!"

Lantry flicked him with a look that held small sympathy. "I guess you'll live," he said briefly. "Your own mistake, getting into the way of a wild bullet." To Bart Williams he added, in a different tone, "We've done all we can right now for Joe Honeycutt. Got the bleeding stopped, at least. Best thing is to keep him quiet. Meanwhile, having started this business we have to go ahead with it."

He turned to Reeves. "I'm glad you're here, Sam. We need Jase Vinson with us, and we need him bad—not only because he and them two boys of his make three more we can use, but more important, we have got to show Arch Caverhill a solid front. You know Jase better than anyone—you'd have the best chance of persuading him. Let's both of us get down to his place, right now, and see what we can do." When Sam Reeves nodded agreement, Lantry turned again to Williams. "Bart, you're in charge here till we get back."

Jim Bannister thought: In charge of two

wounded men, a prisoner, and a couple of scared sentries out in the timber! He saw the same sobering thought reflected in Bart Williams' face; the puncher hesitated before he answered, "All right, Boss. I hope you don't take too long."

"Don't worry," Lantry said. "With or without Vinson, we'll make it back before Broken Spur can send trouble. On the way I'll stop by our place for extra ammunition." He was taking his hat and a fleece-lined jacket from a chair beside the door as he spoke, and motioned for Sam Reeves to move out ahead of him. As he settled the jacket collar in place and started fastening it against the night chill, he paused for another look at Jim Bannister; he frowned and said with some reluctance, "Bart, I don't fancy using a rope on a man, but it might be simpler if you was to tie this fellow up. I don't suppose there's any use putting him on his honor."

"If you mean," Bannister interpreted coldly, "asking my word not to escape if I have the chance—there's no use at all! Would *you* let someone use you to make a bargain with your enemies?" Lantry could seem to find no answer to that, nor could he quite meet Bannister's eyes. His own wavered uncomfortably and slid away; a moment later he was gone, the door slamming behind him.

Left with Bart Williams, Bannister looked at him and saw that the puncher, a man with problems, was considering what his boss had suggested; he was letting a speculative glance rest on that saddle rope, hanging from a peg on the wall. Bannister told the puncher, in a voice tight with anger, "You're not man enough to put that rope on me!"

Williams swung around. Their stares locked.

Then Tobe Munkers spoke up, and despite the whiskey shine that heated up his eyes there was no slurring of his speech, and nothing unsteady about the gunbarrel aimed at Bannister above the edge of the table. "Hell!" Munkers said, and the look on his lantern-jawed face was wolfish in its eagerness. "Don't tie him! Leave the sonofabitch to me!"

Williams said, a trifle dubiously, "You think you can manage him?"

"Hell, yes! I just wish he *would* try something. I owe him!"

The puncher looked at Bannister again, and his eyes went hard. "All right!" he told the man with the gun. "He's yours!"

Chapter X

The return to Broken Spur had been made with scarcely a word spoken between the Caverhills, all the miles from Dunbar. A wall of secrecy between them had finally crumbled, in that moment of revelation in the hotel dining room; but the wall had been a protection for both, and the secret it had guarded was too painful to discuss, now that it was in the open. Silence was easier, and so the silence lay heavily between them—Caverhill gave his angry attention to handling the reins, while Emily sat distantly erect beside him, her hands folded in her lap, her eyes straight ahead.

At long last the carriage, with its escort, rolled into the ranchyard and halted at the steps of the house. Niles helped Emily to alight. When her uncle joined her on the veranda she hesitated there, turning to him, but all she said was a faltering "Good night."

"It's well past midnight. Get a good sleep," he told her gruffly. "We can talk in the morning."

She nodded wordlessly, and left him.

As the surrey was taken on around to the corral Arch Caverhill tramped into the house, but not to bed. He was tired enough, and feeling his age too, he reluctantly admitted; but he was wound too tight for sleep. A drink should help. He dumped hat and coat on the hall table, got a lamp burning, fetched bottle and glass from a cabinet in the living room and poured himself a stiff shot, afterward settling into an armchair with it and staring at the cold ashes of the dead fireplace.

For that time and place he was not a particularly hard-drinking man, nor did he care much for drinking alone. He worked his way stolidly through the contents of his glass, waiting in vain for it to take effect. He had just drained off the last and made a face over it, when there was a knocking at the front door. Grumbling, he hauled himself up and went to answer, carrying the lamp.

Its light showed him, on the porch outside, Wes Niles and four Broken Spur punchers—the ones who had been left in town, and at the Narrows. Niles, who apparently had not been to bed yet himself, told Caverhill, "I seen the light burning. The boys just reported; I figured you'd want to know what happened with that fellow Bonner."

Caverhill nodded impatiently. "Well?"

"It looks like we missed him. Jerry Thatcher," indicating one of the men, "found his horse staked out in that vacant lot in back of the hotel— but Bonner jumped him and bent a gunbarrel over his head. When he come to, the horse was gone and so was Bonner."

Caverhill looked at the puncher. "You hurt bad?"

"Head's a little sore," Thatcher said, touching it gingerly. "Nothing I can't live with." He went on to explain that he'd hunted up the other Broken Spur man who'd been left to search the town for Bonner, and the two of them had decided it was likely he'd ridden out—but whether up or down canyon there was no way to know. In the latter case, the ones who'd been sent to lay a trap should pick him up before he got far. So instead they had headed back for Broken Spur, and when they reached the Narrows they found that the pair stationed there had seen nothing of their man.

Concluding, Wes Niles told his boss, "It don't look from that as though he could have come this way, or at some point the boys would have had him between them. We won't know until later if the others that I sent down canyon, had any better luck. Meanwhile there wasn't any reason why these fellows shouldn't come on in."

"What time is it?"

"Pretty near two a.m."

Caverhill nodded shortly. "All right."

One of the men spoke up in self justification. "It got pretty damn cold, roosting in that canyon!"

"I can imagine." Caverhill looked at Niles. "Get Cookie up and tell him to heat them some coffee."

So Bonner hadn't risen to the bait, he thought as he returned to the living room. He wasn't ready to take odds as to what luck the men posted at the canyon's lower end would have had. For all anyone could say, the bastard might still be right there in Dunbar, maybe having himself a comfortable night's rest in a hotel room and preparing for the next step in his campaign of blackmail. Arch Caverhill cursed him, long and bitterly.

Still in no mood for bed, he settled himself with a stock paper but, his mind being too full of other things, the words he read seemed to make little sense. At last he flung the paper irritably from him. Like a man gingerly probing about his mouth with his tongue in search of a defective tooth, he rummaged his emotions and suddenly discovered what was really bothering him—not so much the threat of the tall stranger and his blackmail, as it was something to do with the scene on the porch of the hotel when Harry Lantry and those other neighbors had come, trying to bargain with him for the Holbrook property.

Damn them, anyway! Lecturing a man and making him feel guilty, when all in the world he had done was try to think of his little girl's happiness, by keeping a promise to himself for an adequate wedding gift!

He flung himself to his feet and took a tour of the silent living room, tugging fiercely at his hatchet-blade of a nose, his face hard as metal. With no fire on the hearth, the room had grown colder; suddenly he needed something to warm

160

him, but rejected the thought of more whiskey. Knowing then what it was he wanted, he turned and strode out through the still house and down the steps and across the yard, to the cookshack.

The lamp's chimney was still warm when he lighted it, and so was the iron coffeepot on the big stove. The ranch cook, already irritable enough at having been rousted out by Wes Niles to take care of the three late-arriving punchers, thrust his head in from his sleeping room to see who was messing around his kitchen; Arch Caverhill flapped a hand at him and ordered gruffly, "Go on back to bed," and the man withdrew.

A couple of pieces of kindling stuffed into the firebox, onto live coals there, quickly had a satisfactory blaze going. It took only a few minutes to bring the coffee up to the temperature he wanted; he filled a china cup, not bothering to use a rag in taking the hot metal of the pot in his rope-scarred fingers, and had a seat at one of the two oilcloth-covered trestle tables where the crew ate their meals.

The coffee was like lye. He drained it off, feeling it could scarcely keep him any more awake than he already was. Afterward he was at the stove for a refill when, surprisingly, he heard riders cantering into the yard. Curious, considering the lateness of the hour, he took his steaming cup to the doorway and looked out. The horsemen came on. There were two of them; they were headed for the house, but when he called out they saw him in the cookshack doorway and swung in that direction.

They came into the light. They were Frank Stroud and his constant shadow, the man called Ridge Decker.

"You're riding late," Arch Caverhill remarked.

Stroud pointed out, "You're up late."

"Just having myself some coffee. Ain't much good but the night's chilly. Join me?"

"Don't mind if I do," Stroud said, and he stepped down, as usual leaving his horse for Decker to tend to. Inside, Caverhill got his guest a cup and filled it. Facing him across the rough table, Stroud drank the coffee black: A man who spent much time around cow camps learned a tolerance for the things he had to put in his stomach. After a moment he asked, a shade too casually, "Is everything all right here?"

"Of course."

The cold eyes studying Caverhill showed their skepticism as the other sparred for an opening. "I couldn't help but wonder," Stroud said evenly. "I knew you'd planned to stay in town till Sunday. When I heard you and Emily had left, without saying a word, it occurred to me there might have been bad news. So, I just thought I'd make sure."

Caverhill interpreted: You mean, you thought you'd check up on me! He was not going to satisfy the curiosity he could see eating badly at the man. "I'm sorry you bothered. It was nothing at all—just a little family matter. Forget it."

"You haven't forgotten," Stroud pointed out, obviously unwilling to let the subject drop, "that in a few hours I'll be a part of this family. I wouldn't like to think there are any problems I can't be allowed to help with."

And Arch Caverhill found himself thinking, You sonofabitch!

It was all he could do to keep himself from saying it aloud, as he watched this man across from him fishing for information. There was a sudden chilling thought: Had the man possibly been hearing rumors—were there hints connected with Emily's past that hadn't yet reached Caverhill's own ears? Could this be the first suggestion from Stroud that he knew of such stories, that he was having second thoughts about the marriage . . . that he maybe wanted out?

The first reaction was bleak dismay, but that gave way almost at once to an anger that shook him until he had to put himself under a stern discipline to hold it in check. Facing Frank Stroud, he suddenly had to admit that he was hard-put to understand why Emily should want to marry him; though to be honest, thinking back he had to remind himself he'd encouraged the match. An ambitious man himself, one who had followed his ambitions and built one of the most important cattle spreads in this part of the

Rockies, he had recognized and approved the signs of ambition in someone else.

The doubts had come later—the growing and irritating sense of this man's arrogance, and a hint of something in him very near to cruelty. Yes, and one more thing, Caverhill thought, frowning at the door as Ridge Decker, having taken care of the horses, entered and sauntered over to the stove for coffee. Caverhill was forced to recognize how much he disliked and even feared Frank Stroud's bodyguard. What sort of man needed a creature like that constantly at his elbow?

Half formed until this moment, the idea suddenly took shape: This marriage could be a mistake!

Well, there was still time. Difficult as it would be, he and his niece were going to have to have a wide-ranging talk, sometime in the hours remaining before Sunday afternoon. Let her hear his increasing doubts; then, if Frank Stroud was still her choice, let the wedding go forward—with Arch Caverhill's blessing.

But until then—

The run of his thoughts was interrupted by a word from Ridge Decker who, from a post he had taken near a window, said briefly, "Rider coming . . ."

Caverhill realized he had been hearing the sound of an approaching horse without actually registering it. It seemed to be a night for late arrivals at Broken Spur; but this one was really pushing his animal. There was a kind of desperate urgency about the sound, that pulled Arch Caverhill to his feet and took him to the doorway. Frank Stroud joined him there.

The rider hit the yard now, at the same pell-mell rush; he reined in at the bunkhouse where Wes Niles lived with the rest of the crew. Caverhill heard the door open, heard voices begin inside. He was already starting across the yard, Stroud following closely, as lamplight showed at a window. By the time he reached there, Wes Niles was coming out and other crewmen were at his heels; the spent horse stood on trailing reins, with drooping head and audibly labored breathing.

Niles had hastily pulled on boots and jeans over his long johns. When he saw his boss he hurried to meet him. "Looks like trouble, Arch," he said. "Could be real bad."

"Let's have it, then!"

The foreman turned and motioned forward the rider who had brought the news. "Here's Ned Anderson to tell you," Niles said. "He and Joe Honeycutt have been holding down that old Holbrook property for us. Tonight they had company. He says it was Lantry and Munkers and some of that crowd—they jumped the place and took it."

"The hell you say!" Caverhill reached and

caught Anderson's arm in a grip that made the man wince. "Are you telling us the truth? You had better be damn sure."

The puncher was still shaken from his experience and from his frantic ride down off the mountain. "Of course I'm sure, Mr. Caverhill! There was a half dozen of 'em, maybe more; I didn't get too good a look—but I know Lantry and Munkers. They just walked in on us before we knew what was happening. There was shooting. I managed to grab a horse and get away, but I think Joe bought it."

"They killed Joe Honeycutt?" Arch Caverhill's voice was like iron.

"I reckon so—I couldn't stick around to make certain. A couple of them come after me but I was able to lose them somehow. . . ."

Wes Niles put in, "He says that's one of their horses he was riding."

"Take a look."

Someone moved the exhausted animal around into the lampglow from the bunkshack window. Niles yelled for the rest to get out of his light, and passed a hand over the ridges of scar tissue on the horse's sweating flank. "A Bar L—that's Lantry's brand, all right."

Caverhill insisted on seeing for himself—he had to have a moment to collect his thoughts. He was angry enough but there were other emotions too, less easy to deal with. Through a numb chill that was more than the coldness of the mountain night he heard Niles saying, "Have these people gone out of their heads? Hell, I can understand them not wanting to give up use of that Holbrook property—but you'd think they'd have sense enough to know, just grabbing a handful of buildings and kicking our line-riders out ain't going to solve anything. Only make matters worse for the lot of them!"

"They know it," Caverhill said grimly. "Harry Lantry does anyway. This is nothing but a gesture of defiance."

Ned Anderson offered, "I heard one of them say, 'It ought to show Arch Caverhill we mean business. . . .'"

"We'll show them who means business!" Niles snapped. "Come daylight. I'll get a rider off to the county seat. Being neighbors and all, maybe they just couldn't figure Broken Spur would call the sheriff in. But, damnit, they're asking for it—they've broken the law, haven't they?"

And then Frank Stroud was saying, "I suggest you forget the sheriff! It would take a week to get him here, and that's too much time to waste on a set of fools! After Sunday, the Holbrook property becomes my responsibility—and *I'll* get them off. That's a promise!"

Something in his voice made Arch Caverhill turn and peer at him sharply, in the dim light. Oh yes, you'd get them off! he thought, in a shock of full understanding. You'd turn Ridge Decker loose on them, and some of your other gun-hands—against men who used to be my friends! That's how you'd solve this problem, isn't it?

He drew a breath; he shook his head. "No! Until Sunday it's still my problem—I won't pass it off on someone else." Without giving Stroud a chance to protest he turned to his foreman. "Get the crew saddled. We're leaving for the mountain."

Niles hesitated. "You mean—now?"

"We'll have daylight in a matter of hours. Meanwhile it might help if I can catch Lantry and the rest off guard, before they're expecting me."

"Shouldn't we send out word and bring some more of our boys in from the camps?"

Caverhill shook his head emphatically. "No time for that. We'll have to make do."

But Frank Stroud, still unsatisfied, confronted the older man to announce, "I'm going up there with you. Whatever you say, I wouldn't feel right otherwise—this is a matter of concern for me, too."

"I dunno . . ." Still there was no good reason to refuse; after probing the man's expression Caverhill said, "Suit yourself." And to Niles: "Have Anderson stay, and Thatcher if his head still bothers him, and maybe one other to help hold down the place for us. The rest will ride—in ten minutes."

In the cubbyhole of a room he called an office, Caverhill got his rifle and six-shooter from the closet where he kept them, checked the loads of both, and buckled on shell belt and holster. He stuffed extra shells for the rifle into a pocket of his windbreaker and went out through the house carrying the saddle gun; he was at the front door when he heard Emily's anxious question from the stairway.

She had come part way down, one hand holding a dressing gown in place. Her feet were bare, her hair let down and worked into a single braid that fell across a shoulder. In the streaky light of the lamp she carried her face was pale, her eyes troubled. "What's happening?" she exclaimed. "All the noise in the yard woke me. Is anything wrong?"

He had no choice but to turn back and face her. He tried to make light of it. "Nothing for you to worry about." But the level regard she put on him demanded an explanation, and he went on briefly, "Some of that bunch that used to lease Tom Holbrook's grass are still acting stubborn about giving it up. Looks like I've got to go up there and talk sense into them."

"With a rifle?" Emily said. "Does it really have to be this way?"

"Arch Caverhill is a man of his word," her uncle told her stubbornly. "You and Frank were promised a fit dowry. I'd like it to be in cash, but

169

as it happens just about everything I own is tied up right now in land and cattle."

She shook her head in protest. "Believe me, it isn't that important. Not if it means—" A movement of her hand indicated the rifle that he held at his side, by the balance.

Arch looked at the weapon, and at her. "There won't be a fight," he assured her, a shade more confidently than he felt. "Harry Lantry is too smart not to know he'd lose it. Far as I'm concerned," he went on, "there's only one thing that matters: You've made your pick. Since you know, without any question, that Frank Stroud is your man—"

"Well, of course," she said quickly—almost too quickly?—and then, after the briefest pause, "I mean—" She broke off, but something in her tone made him look at her sharply.

"Emily . . ."

Before he could say anything more he was interrupted by sounds from the yard outside—the whicker of a horse, the jingling of equipment, and Wes Niles calling, "Arch? You ready?" Caverhill gave an impatient shrug.

On an impulse he reached up and laid a weather-beaten hand on that of his niece, as she stood above him there on the stairs. He told her, with sudden gravity, "Honey, I'm beginning to think maybe we best have a serious talk about things. Soon as I get back . . ." He gave her hand a squeeze and abruptly turned away, taking his white planter's hat from a table by the door.

Carrying the rifle he let himself out, closing the door behind him, and dropped down the porch steps. In the pre-dawn chill his crew, and Frank Stroud, sat their saddles waiting for him, with Wes Niles holding Arch's favorite bay horse by the reins.

Tobe Munkers said tonelessly, "You sonofa-bitch!"

They were the first words anyone had spoken, there in the living room of the old Holbrook place, for the better part of an hour; but to Bannister, at least, the brooding hatred that peered out of Tobe Munkers' sullen and drink-reddened eyes had been something almost tangible. The rancher sat in his chair like a lump, hurt arm tenderly cradled in its sling and the revolver, tin cup and whiskey bottle all within reach. The level of contents in the latter had visibly lowered since Bannister was marched in here, a prisoner. Now Munkers glared across the table at the prisoner and loosed a rolling belch.

He declared, with heavy emphasis, "I still say what you done to me in town only proves I was right!" He passed the back of a hand across his stubbled jaw, and winced to show how sore it still was where Bannister's fist had struck. "I pegged you for a Stroud man, first time I laid eyes on you. But now, by God, I'm supposed to believe that for some reason old man Caverhill wants your hide, to nail to the barn—and I just don't think it makes any sense!" Bannister merely returned the look, without expression. Munkers turned his head. "Bart, do *you* think it makes any sense?"

At the fireplace, Bart Williams straightened from dropping in another length of limbwood that sent a crackling rush of new flame roaring up the chimney. "I ain't too concerned about it making sense," he said briefly. "Harry seems to think it does, and I take Harry's orders."

Tobe Munkers swore and reached for his cup.

Bannister, seated across the table from him, watched as he drained it off. He was wary of the man's unpredictable moods, and thankful for Bart Williams' presence, counting on that as a stabilizing influence to keep the devil inside of Munkers from breaking free. A few minutes ago Williams had stepped out for a tour of the yard, and perhaps to check on the guards. Alone with Munkers, Bannister had had a start when he turned where he stood and saw the man had picked up his gun from the table and had it pointed at him.

"You're too damn fidgety!" Munkers had stated harshly. "You come over here and set, where I can keep an eye on you!" Bannister had had to obey, the eye of the gun-muzzle following every move as he dropped into the chair facing the table. The two had sat and looked at each other, over the gun's barrel that gleamed in the yellow lamplight. It was only when he heard Bart Williams entering, and the gun was again laid upon the table top, that the caught breath came unclogged in Jim Bannister's throat.

Now Munkers put down his empty cup and saw Bannister eyeing the weapon lying between them. His mouth quirked. "I know what you're thinkin'. You'd like nothin' more than to get a hand on that, would you?"

Bannister shrugged. "You could give me the chance, and see."

The suggestion drew a sneering laugh. Munkers looked past him, at Bart Williams. "You hear that? Hell, we got us a joker here! Better try again," he told the prisoner. "It wasn't all that funny."

"I didn't think so myself," Bannister admitted. He was feeling his way with this man, uncertain whether it was less dangerous to attempt bantering with him, or simply to hold his tongue.

There was a groan, just then, from the bedroom where Joe Honeycutt lay. Bart Williams had all along been anxiously concerned about the wounded Broken Spur man; he gave an exclamation now and went hurrying off to investigate. As the doorway curtain dropped in place behind him, Munkers shook his head with a disdainful expression and reached for the whiskey bottle, to refill his empty cup.

This wasn't a moment Jim Bannister could have foreseen, and it almost slipped by him. He'd been in enough tight spots to know that, poor as it was, this was the best chance he was apt to get, and it wouldn't likely come again. Almost before the thought took form, he went into action.

No chance to reach the gun, tantalizingly close but nearer still to Munkers; Bannister didn't try. Instead he brought up both hands, sharply. The heels of his palms struck the table edge and lifted it, toppling it with full force into the man seated across from him. Gun, cup, and bottle all went sliding to the floor; the table, upended, struck Tobe Munkers squarely on that bandaged left arm and dragged a shout of pain from him. And as Bannister surged to his feet, still putting all his weight against the table, both Munkers and the chair he was sitting in were driven over backwards.

Time then seemed to be measured in seconds, as though it had gone into slow motion. The pain in that injured arm should hold the rancher immobilized, for the moment; but there was Bart Williams who would have heard the commotion. Bannister turned, kicking his own fallen chair out of the way as he started for the door. He reached it, fumbled at the latch. Williams was shouting, and he had a glimpse of the curtain shaking wildly as the man fought to paw his way through. Then the door sprang open and Bannister was outside, lacking time even to slam it behind him.

He stumbled in his haste, taking the two plank steps to the ground, and nearly fell sprawling. An uproar inside the house spurred him on as he crossed the dark front wall of the building, ducking below a lighted window. Just before he reached the corner, those shouts broke into the open and a gun went off, startlingly—but he didn't hear the bullet strike, didn't know if it was a wild shot or if he'd actually been seen and targeted.

He got around the corner and as he hauled up there, putting his back against the siding, his boot came down on something that rolled slightly under him; kneeling swiftly he groped and his fingers closed on a solid length of limbwood—kindling somebody must have dropped, on the way to the house with an armload. Bannister grabbed it up—the nearest he could come, just then, to a weapon. He looked around to get his bearings.

The moon had long since set; dawn was not too far off. There was a gray and grainy half-light, and a blanket of ground fog against which buildings and tree trunks and other solid objects bulked blackly. The light could be deceptive, but it was enough for a man with a gun—if Bart Williams was coming, he saw little choice but to stand and meet him. With breath held and the length of wood lifted and ready, he waited.

But there was no hint of anyone approaching. Instead, he heard a new sound—a drum of distant hoofbeats, quickly growing louder. A rider galloped into the yard, and Bannister recognized the voice of Sweeney, the lookout. He had heard the shot and it had tolled him in, demanding to know what was going on.

There in front of the house, Munkers was cussing over his hurt arm and constantly interrupting as Bart Williams explained about the escaped prisoner. "I thought I got a shot at him but I didn't hit anything. But he's around here somewhere," Bannister heard him say, "and it's getting lighter by the minute. The sonofabitch doesn't have a gun; we'll run him down. Why don't you get over to the corral—he might be trying to reach the horses."

"Right!" Sweeney said, and as he went spurring off in that direction Bannister swore a little.

He was free, but in a desperate situation—no horse, no gun, no place to hide, and the grainy light strengthening with each passing moment. He cast about hurriedly. Fairly close at his right hand was the sheltering ridge that rose behind the buildings on the north—a tangle of brush and trees, and down timber knocked over in winter storms. Even afoot he should be able to find at least temporary shelter there. But there wasn't much time to act. Tobe Munkers, coddling that injured arm, was likely no problem; but with two others searching he was bound to be discovered, unless he moved quickly.

Still carrying the club that was his only weapon, he broke out at a run for the timber. He kept low, and tried to put the house between him and the men in the yard; even so, his nerves were tight as he waited for the yell, or the crack of a gunshot, that would tell him he'd been seen. It failed to come, but so intent was he on the danger at his rear that he was nearly surprised from another quarter. Almost too late he caught the warning and flung himself prone, and now the chill ground beneath him carried, all too clearly, hoofbeats of the ridden horse that he had barely glimpsed looming out of the dim half-light, straight ahead.

Bannister had completely forgotten the second lookout, named Clayt Jenkins, who he remembered now had been posted there on the ridge behind the buildings; undoubtedly, like Sweeney, he'd be wanting to check out the goings-on in the ranch yard. Now Bannister hugged the earth, not daring to raise his head or even to breathe as the horse came on at a lope, seemingly straight toward him.

The drum of the hoofs swelled until he could hear the animal breathing, the creak of leather and the swish of dew-wet weeds about its legs.

His muscles bunched. He had to fight an impulse to leap up and run, rather than lie here and let the horseman ride right over him.

Then the rider went by him, perhaps ten yards off to his right. As soon as Jim Bannister judged it safe to move he was up again and running. The ground began to lift under him; then brush was whipping at his clothing. He ducked into its protection, vaulted a fallen log and sank down behind it. In strengthening daylight, with his horse penned out of reach in yonder corral and his gun in the house down there where Bart Williams had left it, he let his breathing settle and asked himself what would happen now.

Chapter XI

Approximately a third of the way up the mountain's flank, a clear spring bubbled out of a rocky cairn; surrounded by a good reach of meadow grass, it made a convenient place for riders to rest and water their mounts before tackling the steeper stretches ahead. Here, as if by tacit prearrangement, the eight horsemen from Broken Spur pulled in and dismounted and slipped their bits, and for the next few minutes the moonless dark was filled with the small sounds of animals muzzling the spring runoff and pulling at the grass. The men lit up cigarettes and walked about, talking in subdued tones, mostly speculating on what lay ahead.

Presently Arch Caverhill gave the order to mount up and be on their way, but before anyone could move Frank Stroud said, "Let's hold it up a few more minutes."

"Whatever for? The night's not getting any younger."

Instead of answering Frank Stroud calmly lit up a cigar from his coat pocket. Looking at his face, expressionless in the glow of the match, Caverhill found himself frowning in puzzlement and a growing resentment. He still did not much like the way Stroud had invited himself along on this mission.

Getting no reply, he was about to repeat his order when a sound of arriving horsemen began to swell upon the night.

They came in at a fast lope—a half dozen, perhaps, by the noise they made. The Broken Spur men went instantly alert; Caverhill heard startled exclamations and he dropped his hand to the chill butt of his holstered gun, as he tried to get a glimpse at the riders. Then they were shaping up out of the darkness, five of them. Ridge Decker's voice came across the night silence: "Frank?"

"Right here," Stroud answered; and as the newcomers pulled in he turned to Caverhill and explained, "I thought more than likely we could use some extra help."

Caverhill felt his temper slipping, at the presumption of the man. He had been puzzled, all along, by the absence of Ridge Decker who always seemed to be at his employer's elbow, but who had disappeared sometime before the group left Broken Spur. Now he understood: Decker must have been dispatched with orders to bring up the rest of Frank Stroud's crew, and to join the party here at the springs—all without a word being said to Caverhill, for his permission or approval.

He was almost at the point of ordering Stroud

to send his men back; but he supposed that would look childish and unreasonable, and he clamped his jaw shut on the unspoken words. After all, no man knew what they were going to find, up at the Holbrook place—he might very well be glad of the extra help before the thing was over. He swallowed his first premonition that no good could come of this, and said roughly, "All right—but don't let them hold us up. We've lost enough time as it is. It will be dawn before we ever get there.

"Let's mount up . . ."

He was right about the time. Long before they reached their destination, the smell and sound of dawn was in the air and the eastern sky, above a black cutout shape of ridges and treeheads, was streaked with growing daylight. Caverhill led his men with increasing wariness, now, approaching the headquarters of the Holbrook property—he would have expected Harry Lantry to have sentries posted as a warning against a possible counter attack, but he saw no sign of any.

And then at last the hollow opened before them and the rough buildings and corral showed in a first wash of sunrise that dimmed the glow of lamplit windows; as they drew in for a look the beginnings of bird song sounded in the trees above their heads.

At his boss' elbow, Wes Niles said, "Ain't that Lantry?"

Caverhill had already spotted him and he nodded without speaking, feeling through all his body the stiffness of night riding and the lack of sleep—Getting old? he wondered fleetingly, and immediately pushed the thought from his head.

It looked as though several horsemen had just ridden in; men and animals were moving about and stirring the layers of ground mist as the riders dismounted and the horses, still under saddle, were being led off to the corral. Caverhill counted ten men, and had no way of knowing if there might not be more inside the house. Even with the addition of Stroud's crewmen, if it came to a fight he couldn't be sure that he had the advantage of numbers.

All at once, he very much hoped it wouldn't come to a fight.

He had halted his party well back, out of sight, while he and Niles went forward to make their inspection. Now Frank Stroud, uninvited, pushed forward to range his animal next to Caverhill's. "Would you look at that?" he said in a tone of scorn. "Not a one has a notion we're anywhere within miles. Pretty damn careless, I'd say."

He had echoed Arch Caverhill's own thought. "If they had sentries, looks like they've been pulled in for some reason."

"It's a bad distance for a rifle; but when the

light gets a little better we ought to pick off a bunch of them before they even know what's happening."

"If that was how we were going to play it," Caverhill agreed. He added firmly, "Only, it isn't."

"What do you have in mind, Arch?" his foreman wanted to know.

"I'm going down there and talk to them."

He saw Wes Niles' face tighten with quick disapproval; and Stroud said impatiently, "Just what good can that do?"

"Boss, he's right," Niles said. "You tried talking to them last night—on the porch at the hotel, remember?—and look what's happened. The thing's gone past the talking stage."

Frank Stroud added, "That rabble has already murdered one of your men," Stroud pointed out. "They'll shoot you down as soon as listen to you."

But Arch Caverhill shook his head. "All the same, I'm going. The rest of you stay here."

"No!" Wes Niles exploded, with a vehemence that surprised his boss. "Arch, I won't let you face that crowd alone! Fire me if you want to— but if you ride down there, the boys and I are riding with you!"

Caverhill wasn't used to open defiance; he started to swell angrily but then he read the stubborn determination in the look his foreman gave him, and for some reason he backed away from it. Scowling he said roughly, "Oh, all right, damn it—anything to end this bickering! But I don't want gunplay, not unless those other people begin it. That clear?"

"Perfectly."

Niles went to give the orders. Caverhill turned to Frank Stroud. "I want you to hold your outfit in reserve. No point letting them know our strength until we have to." He scarcely noticed that Stroud gave him no real answer.

When Niles returned with his punchers, Caverhill looked them over in the half-light of dawn filtering through the trees. They were well armed, with belt pistols, and all but a couple had a saddle gun in the boot. Caverhill repeated his stern warning: "I don't want to see a weapon out of its holster unless I give the order." He stared at each one until he got a nod of understanding.

The sun was high enough now that its light spilled down the eastern ridge and made the protected hollow glow with it, the drifts of ground mist turning to pearl before melting under the warming rays. Frank Stroud and Ridge Decker and their four riders looked on in silence as the men from Broken Spur left the trees and, with Caverhill and his foreman in the lead, started down the wagon track that led to the buildings below them.

They rode without hurry, watching the activity

at the house. The last of the horses had been shoved into the pen, still with their saddles on. The men stood about in serious talk; sunlight shone on the bluish metal of rifle barrels in the hands of some of them.

Suddenly Wes Niles told his boss, "Watch it!"

"I'm watching . . ."

They had been seen as they came out onto the open floor of the hollow. All at once the men at the house broke and scattered, much like a yard full of chickens at sight of a hawk. A couple who were near the barn ducked inside, a third sought cover behind a corner of the corral; but most headed instinctively for the house itself. Only Harry Lantry stayed put and watched the nearing horsemen, with hand lifted to shield his eyes against the sun. Somebody grabbed at his arm and tried to haul him toward the house, but Lantry shook him off.

As that flurry of activity ceased, quiet returned but now the dooryard was empty except for Lantry, standing bareheaded and defiantly alone. Behind him, a window was run up with a quick squealing and a gun-barrel dropped across the sill. At once Wes Niles turned and flung an order, and the men behind him abruptly reined for a stand of trees to the right of the trail: They would have some protection there from rifles hidden in the house.

Arch Caverhill and his foreman kept going, to halt finally facing Harry Lantry. For a moment nobody spoke. Caverhill's animal stomped a time or two and shook out its mane. That rifle barrel still poked menacingly across the windowsill, pointed in Caverhill's direction, and there was the gleam of another one over by the corner of the corral where even the saddle horses stood motionless as statues, as though waiting for something to happen. Chimney smoke rose in a lazy blue pencil-line above the roof of the house; the timbered ridge behind smoked with tendrils of mist rising through the trees.

Caverhill punched the hat to the back of his head. "Well, Harry!" he said loudly. "You've stirred up a real mess, ain't you? And Joe Honeycutt killed, in doing it—that's murder, Harry!"

Lantry's head jerked sharply. "It ain't true!" he exclaimed. "I dunno what you've heard, but your man's going to live—believe me! Of course, it don't make me any less sorry that someone had to get hurt."

"Well, at least I'm glad to know about Honeycutt," the other conceded. "We'll hope to God you're right. But you should have known something like that was bound to happen. Now, are you ready to talk sense?"

"You bring an army against us," Harry Lantry retorted harshly, "and then ask us to talk!"

"Do you call eight men an army?"

"Eight? What about *them?*" Lantry flung up a pointing arm.

Caverhill turned his head for a look and swore under his breath. "That damned Stroud! I told him—"

He broke off and angrily watched a line of horsemen moving, in single file, down the face of a ridge toward a shallow wash, lined with willow and scrub, where they apparently meant to take cover. It looked as though they had found a stock trail of some kind, for they were descending at a fair clip, weaving in and out through trees and boulders, from shadow into sunlight, with Stroud and Ridge Decker in the lead. Caverhill told himself, with a sour grimace, that he might have known Frank Stroud would follow instructions only if it pleased him.

Harry Lantry said, "Well, there it is, Arch. If you and Stroud want war—you can damn well have it!"

Exasperated, Arch Caverhill turned on him. "Nobody wants a war—but if you don't watch your step you *may* force me to call the law in here! Damnit, I'm asking you: Would you really want to have the sheriff put you off this property?"

"You'd do that?" Lantry flared back at him, fist trembling as he lifted it. "To men that were your friends? Arch, you know we can't last without our summer range. Oh, there may be a few can pick up the pieces and make a fresh start somewhere; but it's a little too late for some of us to be climbing off the floor again!" He added bitterly, his mouth twisting, "Or am I wasting my breath? Can anybody fixed as well as you are have an idea at all what I'm talking about!"

Arch Caverhill stiffened. "Maybe you think I ain't been on the floor a few times, my own self!" he retorted. "I always climbed back up."

"But could you do it *now?* You and me—we ain't as young as we used to be, Arch. And it gets a little hard."

For some reason he couldn't answer that. Looking at Harry Lantry, standing there in the thin sunlight, it was as though he saw, for the first time, the sparse white hair and sunken cheeks and gnarled hands of a man he had always thought of as strong and hale and vigorous. Time had been doing something to the solid line of his shoulders; as with Arch Caverhill himself, he'd had no sleep last night and it was plain that, like an old man, he was feeling it. The appalling thought crushed home: If this is true of Harry, it has to be true of *me!*

Now Wes Niles said, with a younger man's impatience, "We're just wasting time. All the talk in the world can't change the fact you people are breaking the law. You keep on, and sure as hell somebody is going to wind up—"

He was cut short by the report of a rifle, that

ripped the stillness and sent confusing echoes rolling about the timbered ridge faces.

Mud that had been dislodged by the strike of the bullet gouted up within an inch of Harry Lantry's boot and drove him stumbling back, as he cried out in alarm. And Niles, who owned quicker reflexes than his employer, saw at once what was sure to follow; he gave his mount a kick and a jerk of the reins that started it pivoting, ramming into Caverhill's bay. Reaching, he caught the other horse by its bridle and pulled it on around. Then both were galloping for timber cover, as the guns inside the house answered that first startling shot with a volley.

As quickly as that, the thing had broken apart in violence.

When he reached the trees, Arch Caverhill was white from shock and fairly trembling with anger. His riders who had already taken cover there had left their saddles, and spread out to hug the tree trunks and return the fire. By now a continuing barrage from both sides was rattling out across the morning sunlight; bullets clipped pine branches overhead. Still in saddle, Caverhill threw a furious look over his men and cried, "Stop this!" One or two who could hear him above the shooting obeyed his order, but they looked at him blankly as he demanded harshly, "Who did it? Who let off that first shot?"

Someone exclaimed, "It wasn't none of us!" and Roy Karns told his boss, "It came from over there, Arch—that wash yonder, where Stroud and his men are holed up."

"The hell you say!" Caverhill's head whipped around and he saw bursts of powdersmoke, proving Stroud's men were into the fight, above the scrub growth.

Wes Niles, having dismounted, hurried over now and caught at the old man's sleeve, anxiously. "Arch, you better get down! You make too good a target!" Swearing at him, Caverhill batted his hand away. Suddenly, jaw set firm, he yanked the horse around and sunk the spurs. The animal leaped and settled into a gallop.

Caverhill scarcely heard his foreman's cry of protest, behind him; he gave little thought to being exposed to those rifles at the house, even when something sang past his head with a sound like a hornet—it was a fairly long range, to expect any of Harry Lantry's men to hit a moving target. His bay leaped the double ruts of the wagon track, dipped into a swale and lifted out of it again. And then he was close enough to make out the men crouched in the bottom of the wash, their horses bunched nearby. He dropped down the crumbling bank and hauled rein in a shower of dirt, calling out for Frank Stroud.

Stroud came with Ridge Decker at his heels, the

latter carrying a smoking saddle gun. The rancher looked unruffled by what was going on around him. He said reprovingly, "That was pretty risky, what you just did. One lucky bullet is all those people would have needed."

Caverhill dismissed Stroud's remark with an impatient gesture. But next moment a bullet struck the lip of the draw and spattered them all with grit, and that prompted him belatedly to swing a leg across and step down from his exposed position in the saddle. Powdersmoke was beginning to lie in drifts along the still air of the draw, pungent in the nostrils. The bay tossed its head uneasily but Arch Caverhill kept a firm grip on the reins. "If you had stayed where I told you," he said, fury in his voice, "this wouldn't have happened."

The cold eyes seemed to be studying him, measuring the extent of his anger. Stroud said, "I dispute that. Any fool could have seen they were spoiling for a fight."

"But they never started this one! I understand the first shot came from *here.*"

"Well, yes, it's true enough. One of the boys was sighting in his piece. He was nervous and he overestimated the trigger pull. It was purely an accident."

"Was it?" In his present anger Caverhill didn't really care that the question was a challenge, virtually calling the other man a liar. He turned away without waiting for an answer, or seeing how Stroud's jaw muscles tightened as the barb sank home.

The firing continued, the ranch buildings being hit from two directions while answering spurts of powder-smoke, at the windows and in the barn entrance and at places around the yard, showed where Lantry's followers had dug in. If anything, the fight was getting hotter—and as he looked around him, Caverhill had a crawling conviction that these men of Stroud's actually enjoyed such work. Nearby he saw one fellow squeeze off a shot and lever the empty shell from his weapon, actually showing his teeth in a grin as he bragged to no one in particular, "I sure as hell dusted one of 'em that time!"

Turning back to the man's employer, Arch Caverhill said, "Frank, tell them to quit firing!"

Stroud merely looked at him, making no move to comply. The man next to Caverhill must have heard the order but he ignored it; he brought his rifle in position, squinted along the barrel and calmly fired again. And at that, something in Arch Caverhill seemed to snap.

He whirled and seized the heated metal tube. Caught by surprise, the man didn't fight for it but let him snatch the weapon from his hands, turn, and fling it as far as he could, end-for-end up over the side of the wash. After that Caverhill was facing Stroud and his voice crackled as he said, "I won't tell you again! I want this stopped. I mean now!"

"You aren't backing down?" Stroud demanded sharply. "You don't intend giving in to them? Arch, I'm surprised at you!"

"I'm surprised at myself," Caverhill retorted, "when I realize what I've been doing! Those people are desperate. I just wouldn't let myself admit it, but they finally drove it home. Because, they're right! They lose this grass, and every one of them is ruined. They were my friends once, and damn it, I can't do it to them!"

A harsh edge honed the other man's tone. "But the property's spoken for! It's been promised to me—" He seemed to think twice, and amended that: "It's been promised to Emily . . ."

"Emily will understand. At least I'm hoping so. If *you* don't—" Arch Caverhill shook his head. "Well, maybe part of the trouble has been that I was just too anxious nothing should sidetrack this wedding. Maybe I'm not so anxious any more!"

Abruptly he turned back to his horse, found the stirrup and lifted his spare, iron-hard figure into the saddle. Frank Stroud demanded, "What do you think you're going to do?"

With the sound of the rifle fire crackling all about, Caverhill looked down at him. "Right now," he said, "I'm going out there and tell Harry Lantry and the rest they can

193

keep their Lease—on any terms they want!"

"You're making a mistake!" But Arch Caverhill's only answer to that was a kick of the spurred boot, that sent his animal scrambling up the bank of the wash and out into the open.

Stroud was left staring after him, with a look of iron. He turned his head then and found Ridge Decker watching, as though waiting for instructions. Neither spoke. Frank Stroud gave his man the briefest of nods; it was enough. Unhurried, Decker deliberately kicked out a toe hole in the dirt and used it to hoist himself, so he could rest both elbows on the draw's edge and line up his rifle on the retreating figure of Arch Caverhill.

The old man was suddenly having trouble, out there. If he had thought he could ride straight in on the buildings, perhaps with a palm lifted in the Indian sign of peace, he was clearly mistaken. A truce flag might have helped, if he'd had one. But there was no letup at all in the firing from the house and he pulled rein, uncertainly.

And then something happened.

The bay, taking fright—perhaps even stung by a wild bullet—reared under him suddenly and he had to fight it around in a tight circle, trying to get it settled. It was into this blur of movement that Ridge Decker squeezed off his shot. Arch Caverhill doubled forward; the frantic, circling motion of his animal flung him bodily out of the saddle.

The wide-brimmed planter's hat went sailing from his head when he fell, loosely, as only a dead man can fall.

Chapter XII

Wes Niles was first to reach his boss, using the stock of a smoking rifle to goad speed out of his mount. Even before he threw the reins and leaped down, he saw the blood slowly soaking the back of the old man's windbreaker and knew, with a cold certainly, that Arch Caverhill was dead.

Everyone seemed to know it. The firing had thinned and petered out and now an eerie stillness lay over the hollow; Caverhill's bay had run off a little distance and then fallen to grazing as though nothing had happened. It didn't take the signal from Niles to bring his men hurrying. Having given them their orders he mounted again, sliding his saddle gun into the boot with a savage thrust, and rode to confront Harry Lantry who had emerged from the house and stood waiting, empty-handed and motionless.

Niles leaned a forearm on the pommel as he stared at Lantry, and at the other men who had followed him into the yard. He said, with suppressed fury trembling in his voice, "Well, you did it! Damn the lot of you—Arch is dead. And you murdered him!"

Harry Lantry's face was ashen, his eyes haunted, his mouth a tragic line. "He's really dead?" He looked past Niles, to where the Broken

Spur men were gently and carefully lifting their employer's broken body from the ground. "Wes, I swear to God—we never intended anything like this!"

"One of you must have," Niles retorted harshly. "He was plugged dead center!"

"In a fight," the older man pointed out, in the same lifeless tone, "anything can happen. I have no idea which of our men fired that shot. I won't quit until I know!"

Wes Niles shrugged. "What's the difference? Knowing won't bring him back. And you were all part of it. The sheriff's gonna say you're equally responsible." But then, despite his bitter anger Wes Niles found himself softening enough to add, "Were any of your boys hurt?"

Lantry dully shook his head. "We were lucky. Sam Reeves had his cheek cut by flying glass when a window light got busted. Bullet nicked one of my crew along the ribs but didn't chew him up too bad . . ." He looked at his scuffed and dusty boots. He drew a shuddering breath. "We'll be pulling out now. Please tell Emily I'm damned sorry for the way this ended. We all are!"

And then, in bleak silence, they looked on as four of the Broken Spur men filed by and into the house, grimly carrying Arch Caverhill's limp body. Afterward, Lantry's followers broke up and began a dispirited movement in the direction of the corral where their saddled horses were penned.

Wes Niles turned as Frank Stroud came up, with Decker and all the rest of his crew. To Stroud's question he answered curtly, "Fight's over. These people are leaving. I've sent for a wagon to take Arch back down with us. I'll be posting a guard to make sure nothing more happens here."

Stroud said, with the faintest hint of scorn, "After last night, I ain't sure you got the men to do it. But a couple of my boys can stay and lend a hand."

Wes Niles looked over Stroud's silently waiting men; he couldn't keep his distaste for them from putting a rough edge on his refusal. "Thanks just the same!" he grunted. "I reckon we'll make out . . ."

For a moment the antagonism between these two men flared and hung nakedly between them. Stroud's jaw set, the muscles bunching, and the man's lips scarcely moved as he said with elaborate politeness, "Yes, Mr. Niles. You go right ahead and do what you think you have to. We'll be talking again later." Unspoken was the promise behind the words: In a few hours, when I'm the new master of Broken Spur!

Stroud didn't have to voice the threat. Abruptly he pulled rein, turning his horse. His men fell in behind him and Wes Niles watched them spur away up the wagon track and out of the hollow, with bitterness in his eyes.

He turned back. Under the surveillance of the Broken Spur crew, the men who had usurped the Holbrook property were preparing now to evacuate; they moved in a stunned silence, roping their horses from the corral and riding slowly out of the yard with the look of men who still could not understand what had happened. Niles' own thoughts were locked in turmoil and it was a moment before he registered something he saw at the corral. But then it hit him, hard, and jarred an oath from him.

He spurred forward. Bart Williams was walking toward the pen; Niles came up from behind, leaned and caught him by a shoulder, spinning him around. "All right!" he gritted, as the puncher caught his balance and started to swear at him. "That dun horse, with the centerfire saddle: Mister, if you know you better tell me and tell me quick! What's it doing here? Where's the yellow-haired sonofabitch who belongs to it?"

Jim Bannister had had what amounted to a grandstand seat for the gunbattle, having climbed the ridge to a point where a rock spill had sheared off a stand of timber to give him a view over the buildings, and the pocket where they stood. With nothing obstructing his line of sight, he was able to see whatever went on almost as clearly—in that crystal-sharp mountain morning, alive with the sounds of birds—as if he had the glasses that were still cased on his saddlehorn.

He had seen Harry Lantry return with reinforcements, and watched Bart Williams and Tobe Munkers come hurrying out to meet him, obviously to report the escape of their prisoner. There had been some excitement over that, to be quickly forgotten when the riders from Broken Spur, led by Arch Caverhill himself—easily identifiable by that low-crowned, white planter's hat he always seemed to wear—appeared suddenly on the wagon track leading down to the buildings.

Bannister had watched the rest scatter into hiding while Lantry himself went to confront the Broken Spur owner; afterward, when the fighting started, he saw every spurt of rifle smoke, drifting and dispersing, and heard the mingled rattling of gunfire and the frightened squeals of horses in the pen. But for Bannister there was nothing to do but watch—without a weapon, unable to interfere if he had wanted to.

And so it was that he saw Ridge Decker coolly and deliberately drop Arch Caverhill out of the saddle, with the bullet that brought the fight to a sudden halt. He was left shaken by the callousness of it—and by a swelling anger.

As he continued to watch, it soon became clear to Bannister that neither the Broken Spur crew, nor the ones holed up in the buildings, understood just how Caverhill had died. From the way Harry Lantry and his people filed into the open, empty-handed and with the fight knocked out of them, they obviously held themselves to blame; they moved like men weighted down with guilt. Bannister watched Caverhill's body carried into the house, watched Stroud confer briefly with Wes Niles and after a moment take his crew and ride out, as though satisfied with the victory. Lantry's men were already at the corral, mounting up, their actions the wooden movements of defeat.

Suddenly, Bannister stiffened.

The dun horse! Somehow he had forgotten that Wes Niles, at least, knew it by sight from having seen it in the Broken Spur yard, yesterday afternoon. Now he had seen it again! Bannister watched him collar Bart Williams, saw him gesture toward the corral and saw Williams, answering, indicate the ridge behind the buildings. Minutes later, with the rest of them gone and no one left down there but his own crew, Niles yelled an order and shortly he was leading them in a charge straight at the slant of the hill. Their intentions couldn't have been clearer.

Bannister had to resist lunging to his feet— here, he was reasonably well hidden and he knew he would have no hope of escape once he

202

showed himself or started running. So he kept low, holding where he was even when it seemed he could look down the flaring nostrils of one of the Broken Spur horses which came toiling directly toward him. Less than a hundred feet from his hiding place, the spill of timbers and fallen boulders made it necessary for the rider to pull wide and hunt a better ascent. Climbing, he passed within yards of Bannister. Branches and brush snapped as the horse shouldered through; moments later, the line of Broken Spur men had swept past and as Bannister listened to them, working their way on up the hill, the sound of their passage slowly began to fade.

It occurred to him they must have thought they were after a man trying to escape ahead of them on foot—they'd naturally suppose anyone would have used the cover the gunbattle gave, to put some kind of distance between him and his enemies. Now, while they blundered on hunting him, he should have at least a few minutes before they realized their mistake. It was a slight break in his favor, for once, and Bannister meant to take advantage of it.

He came down off the hill cautiously, searching for danger but seeing only the movement of three saddled horses remaining in the pen, and a drift of smoke still lazing up from the mud chimney of the house. As he approached the corral the dun spotted him and lifted its head; the other pair circled away when he went through the bars. There was water and feed, and the dun should be rested and in shape for travel. But like these other animals, it was still upset by the gunfire that had torn the morning apart. Bannister spoke to settle it. Saddle and bridle and blanket roll were all in place. He checked the cinch, then took the reins and started leading it toward the gate.

That was too much for those other frightened horses. As they skittered out of his path one shook its mane and loosed a shrill whinny of alarm, that cut across the morning stillness. Bannister swore. He thought the searchers on the ridge must surely have heard that.

He fastened the gate behind him and, hurriedly mounting, rode to the house for his gun.

He was thinking that, what with Joe Honeycutt lying in the house critically wounded, Wes Niles would probably have left at least one man here; so he was not too much surprised, after the disturbances at the corral, that someone should come slamming out to investigate just as he rounded the corner into view of the door.

It was Gilson, who'd traded shots with him last evening in the hotel dining room. He hadn't struck Bannister then as much of a gunfighter, judging from the way he'd broken and run after a single exchange of shots. He had a gun in his hand now but when he saw a horseman closing on him he merely braked in midstride, staring, and only belatedly thought to raise the weapon. That was too late. A muscled shoulder of the dun struck the man and spun him, flinging him against the rough wall with an impact that made Bannister wince to see it. Gilson bounced off, loose in all his joints. He hit the ground and lay with his chest working, fighting to gain the breath that had been knocked out of him.

Bannister left the saddle. He saw the revolver Gilson had dropped and, not knowing if there might be still another Broken Spur man inside the house, grabbed it up. Quickly, then, he mounted the stoop and, with the captured gun ready, stepped through the doorway.

Gilson had been alone. The house had taken a battering, during the dawn siege; broken glass, from windows knocked out during the fighting, crunched underfoot. A sound of painful breathing took him into the bedroom where the hurt man, Joe Honeycutt, looked at him with glazed eyes that apparently saw nothing. Out in the main room, chairs had been drawn together and here Bannister found the blanket-covered figure of Arch Caverhill, waiting to be hauled down to Broken Spur for burial. Looking at the motionless shape, he bleakly pondered the treachery that had put it here—and thought again that he apparently was the only witness who could tell what had really happened. But the pressure of his own concerns turned him away.

By some lucky chance, no one had removed his six-shooter from the shelf where he had seen Bart Williams put it. Bannister retrieved it, leaving Gilson's weapon in its stead. He checked the loads and dropped the gun into holster.

Afterwards, feeling keenly the passage of time, he went back outside, carefully closing the door. Gilson was sitting in the dirt, head hanging; he didn't even look up, and Bannister didn't bother him. He mounted the dun and, without any more loss of precious time, left that place.

Chapter XIII

He rode into Dunbar warily, mindful of the four riders Wes Niles had sent off down-canyon last evening to lay a trap for him—he probably wouldn't know them by daylight and he didn't want to take any chance of blundering into them.

It was taking a real risk to come this way at all. He didn't have any doubts that Wes Niles would have sent someone after him, having checked back with Gilson and learned that Bannister had eluded pursuit and made off safely with his horse and a gun. He'd made some effort to bury his tracks, but there was scarcely any use in that—after all, since he wasn't taking the high trail over the pass it left only the canyon route out of this country. And Niles would know that as well as Bannister did.

The sun stood at noon. The canyon had filled with a drowsy heat that put dancing waves of refraction above the rooftops, the murmur of the river in its rocky channel making a half-heard background. Bannister's last solid meal had been in the private dining room of the hotel, the night before, and the smell of coffee and frying meat that drifted to him now through the open door of an eatery was tempting; but he resolutely passed by.

He had business to accomplish here. He was taking a chance to do it and he wanted to get it done as quickly as possible, and then leave. The strip of jerky from his saddlebag that he had been chewing on would have to hold him, until he was able to make camp and break out his trail rations.

No casual observer, watching him pull rein before the stone-and-log structure that housed the jail and marshal's office, would likely have guessed the tension in him. He moved deliberately but he was carefully testing the street quiet as he stepped down and tied the dun. A settling of his shoulders, a reassuring touch of the gun in his holster; that was all. After that he crossed the dry plankings of the sidewalk and, finding the door unlocked, opened it and entered.

The jail was a sturdy one, for a town as small as this, its walls solid and thick and the windows set high. The office was small, sparsely furnished, neat; a door at the rear would lead to the cellblock. Seated behind a flat-topped desk, a newspaper spread open before him, Marshal Blackman looked at his visitor without expression on his thin-lipped, bearded face. "Well?" he said sharply. "Come in."

Bannister closed the door and approached the desk, and the cold eyes that seemed to study him. "Bonner, eh?" The marshal gestured to a straight-backed chair across from him; his caller took it and laid his hat in his lap. Blackman said shortly, "Well?"

Jim Bannister began, "I wasn't sure you'd remember me, from yesterday evening—"

"I remember! I'd not likely forget, not after the stir you raised."

"You mean, when I wouldn't let that fellow Munkers go berserk?" But the lawman shook his head.

"Oh, no. I certainly couldn't complain about *that*—whatever reason you might have had for doing it. I'm talking about afterward: at the hotel, with Arch Caverhill apparently trying to tear the place apart to get his hands on you. *That's* what has this town buzzing—and I haven't been able to answer anybody's questions, because the whole thing was finished before I even got word of it, or could get involved."

"No reason you should. Nobody got hurt; no laws were broken."

"Are you sure?" Frowning, Blackman pulled open a drawer of his desk, took out a plug of tobacco and worried off a cheekful. He worked it between his jaws as he laid the plug on the desk and looked thoughtfully at the other man. "I admit," he said finally, "I don't actually know but what that's the truth. Still, it don't stop the questions—*or* the rumors. I ought to tell you, we're very big on rumors; it's the way of a small town."

Bannister let him have it: "I wonder if you've heard rumors yet this morning, about a gunbattle up the mountain—the Holbrook place?"

Blackman ceased chewing, the wad of tobacco distending a cheek. "No," he said. "I ain't heard anything like that."

"You will, and before the day is many hours older. That kind of story doesn't take long to spread."

"Maybe you're here to help spread it."

"What I came to tell you isn't rumor, but fact!" Bannister assured him. "What I saw with my own eyes."

That other stare locked with his, a long moment. "Tell it, then," the lawman ordered, his jaws working again. "But start at the beginning."

"You could say that it began last night," Bannister told him. "When Tobe Munkers' friends talked you into setting him loose."

"I only locked him up for his own good, until he sobered. And Harry Lantry and the others promised they'd get him out of town and keep him out."

"But they didn't tell you what they had in mind, that they needed his help with." And with no more preface than that Jim Bannister went on to tell about last night—leaving himself out of it, keeping to the events that led to the dawn raid and ended with Ridge Decker's treacherous shooting of Caverhill. There was a long silence when he had finished; Merl Blackman, staring at him fiercely, rubbed a knuckle across his close-cropped beard. He turned his head and used the brass spittoon that sat beside his desk.

He said, "How much of that do you expect me to believe?"

"If you don't believe Caverhill is dead," Bannister said, "all you have to do is wait awhile—you'll be getting the word soon enough. On the other hand, if what you don't believe is that it was deliberate murder, then you have only my word for it."

Those eyes continued to study him. "I dunno if you realize it, but you've left out a few things. Just what the hell were *you* doing up there? How did you happen to be a witness, if you weren't involved yourself?"

Bannister had known that question was coming. He took his time answering it, and carefully chose his words. "I'll say no more than this: I came to you because I was a man with a problem. Someone had to be told how Arch Caverhill died. You strike me as a fair man. I was sure you'd at least hear me out—and you'd remember, whether you believed me or not."

The other was shaking his head before he even finished. "I'm only a town officer, Bonner," the marshal pointed out bluntly. "Whatever I might or might not believe—on your unsupported word!—I still don't have jurisdiction over anything that happens on the mountain. All I could do is call the sheriff in from the county seat, and let you repeat your story to him."

"Then call him—only, you'll have to repeat it yourself because I won't be here. I'm leaving."

Blackman straightened slightly in his chair. He started to say, "I don't think so!" But the speech died on his tongue when Bannister lifted the hat from his lap, and showed him the six-shooter he had been holding with its hammer eared back, its muzzle aimed squarely at the marshal's chest.

"Don't touch the gun in that drawer," Bannister said, and at once the hand that had started toward it went motionless. Now he reached and slid the newspaper from the desk, and revealed beneath it an all-too-familiar sheet of stiff cardboard—a reward notice, bearing his own woodcut likeness and description.

Bitter eyes on the tall man's face, voice toneless, the marshal said, "What gave me away?"

"It just didn't jibe," Bannister told him. "You were too willing to let me talk, when it was clear you didn't believe a word. That told me you were playing me along, trying to decide how to handle me . . ." He rose and, still covering his prisoner, went around the desk, now he could see the glint of the handgun in the drawer Blackman had opened. He left it there, simply kneeing the drawer shut, and told the marshal, "Get to your feet."

Blackman's face was tight with anger but he obeyed, and let himself be herded at gunpoint through the door at the back of the office. This opened into the cellblock, made up of three barred cubbyholes. Bannister had found a key on the desk, and he unlocked one and shoved his prisoner inside. When the door had been slammed and the lock tested, the two men eyed each other through the bars.

"I don't think anyone's going to hear you yelling, Marshal," Bannister said. "Not through walls as thick as these. Sooner or later somebody will find you and let you out. Meanwhile I suggest you take it easy—and while you're at it, think over what I tried to tell you.

"Because, even if I can't hope to prove how Arch Caverhill died—I swear to you every word you heard from me was the truth!"

The cold eyes snapped with scorn. "You're seriously calling another man a murderer? *You,* Bannister?" The words struck like a whiplash, and stung a hot flush into the tall man's cheeks. He met the look; his mouth tightened. Without another word Jim Bannister wheeled around and strode from the cellblock, his boot-heels striking up sharp echoes.

All right—so it had been a hopeless undertaking, to approach Merl Blackman! Still, he couldn't have simply ridden away from here—not carrying his burden of knowledge about the death

213

of Arch Caverhill, not without at least trying to put it somewhere on the record. Well, he could say he had tried . . . and come near to disaster. He saw absolutely nothing more he could do.

He closed the cellblock door, glad of the heavy construction that made this building almost soundproof, and dropped the big key onto Blackman's desk. The dodger, that the marshal must have discovered in his file drawer, still lay among the papers there; almost as an afterthought Bannister picked this up, folded it small and shoved it into a pocket of his coat—no sense leaving it, for curious eyes to see and recognize his picture. As he was crossing the room to let himself out he heard a beginning sound of hoofs and wheels in the street. He closed the office door behind him, and at the rail where his horse was tied paused to watch a stage and four-horse hitch come rocking into town, leaving a moil of dust where it had broken out of the lower canyon.

Ready to mount, he stiffened suddenly, staring across his saddle at a face he saw in a window of the coach.

Surprise and recognition held him motionless, until the billow of dust and grit spun up by the iron-tired wheels engulfed him and he had to duck away from it. When he looked again the coach was already pulling up in front of the station, farther along the street. It rocked on its leather thoroughbraces while the dust slowly settled, amid the usual flurry of activity.

Bannister turned and gave one last, regretful look toward the opening of the lower canyon, which offered him the quickest route of escape from this place. After that, stepping into the saddle, he swung back instead in the direction of the station, where the driver was climbing down from his perch and the passengers starting to alight.

A man from the station had hurried out to begin unloading the rear luggage boot. The one he had seen through the window—a spare, well-dressed figure who wore a duster over his traveling clothes—stood to one side wiping dirt from an expensive-looking Homburg, while waiting to reclaim his luggage. It was handed to him, a small canvas grip, and as he turned away with it he glanced up and saw Jim Bannister, who had halted the dun a few paces away. His smooth features masked any hint of surprise; he revealed nothing at all when their eyes met and Bannister, leaning slightly while he pretended to smooth the saddle leather, said quietly, "You looking for me?"

Sharp blue eyes met his. The man nodded, started to speak; Bannister cut him off. "Not here. Get yourself a horse from the livery and ride up the canyon. I'll be watching for you."

After the briefest hesitation, the other gave

a nod to show he understood. At the signal Bannister straightened and touched the dun with his heel. As he rode unhurriedly up the street, nothing in his manner would have suggested the pressures on him, or the trouble he'd been forced to leave locked in a cell of Dunbar's jail.

The sound of a horse approaching began to make itself heard, above the restless water and the movement of wind through this narrow canyon. Jim Bannister got quickly to his feet and dropped the cigarette he had been smoking, ground it into the dirt with his boot-toe. Grown tense with waiting, he said aloud, gruffly, "It's about time!" Surely more than enough time for the man from the stagecoach to have picked up a livery mount, and ridden this short distance.

Bannister, accordingly, worked his way downward, reaching a point where he could push aside a screen of branches and get a look without showing himself. Moments later the horseman appeared around a turn—but it was a figure in the sweated range hat and Levi's and scarred brush jacket of a ranch hand. He pulled quickly back, and swore under his breath as he watched the rider pass his hiding place and disappear on up the canyon.

He could see no reason at all for the delay.

There'd been another rider by, only minutes

earlier, traveling at a good pace but from the opposite direction. Whatever mission had sent him heading for Dunbar looked like an urgent one; Bannister speculated he might have been bringing word of the fight on the mountain, and perhaps orders to fetch back the doctor for Joe Honeycutt or someone else suffering from a bullet wound. In that case it wasn't hard to imagine the bombshell that would soon be exploding, when news of Arch Caverhill's passing hit that town that had lain so long under his shadow, and the shadow of Broken Spur . . .

Another sound, now—the sing of wheels and leisurely pacing of a horse between the shafts of a buggy. The rig came in sight, tooling along at a comfortable and unhurried pace, and he saw the figure seated alone beneath the leather top. He looked more closely and recognized the man he was waiting for. With an angry grimace and a shake of the head, Bannister dropped down the remaining distance to the level of the trail, and stepped into the open.

Boyd Seldon brought his rented vehicle to a stop. In a poor temper, Bannister said, "I never expected you'd be hiring a rig!"

"You know perfectly well I'm no horseman," the Western Development Corporation official told him.

"The whole idea was to find a place where we could talk without being seen or interrupted.

A contraption like this isn't going to make it easier."

Selden started to comment, "You don't make the situation here sound encouraging," but Bannister cut him off, saying, "Well—wait up a minute."

He climbed back to where he had left the dun—a secluded and carefully chosen spot for a rendezvous, but not one where they could take a buggy. So, mounting, he returned to the road and gestured for the other to follow. They continued on for some minutes before he found a place that suited him, a shallow cove of rocks and scrub—no real cover, but at least they could talk there without being too conspicuous to anyone passing. He waved the buggy into this, and dismounted while Selden climbed out and began to move about, stretching muscles still stiff from the long stage ride over the mountains from Denver. The syndicate man removed his Homburg, mopped dust from a smooth-shaven and shrewd businessman's face. He said, "All right—what's the secrecy about? What's wrong?"

For answer Bannister simply took the reward dodger from his pocket and handed it over. Selden did no more than glance at it. "I see . . . Well, the way this State is plastered with these things, I suppose there's no getting away from them. Where did you find this one?"

"On the desk in the town marshal's office! I

left him locked in one of his own cells. Probably somebody will have found him by now," he added. "The word will be out and I may not have much time—So, what's brought you here?"

"A new development," Selden told him, "since I wrote you. By the way, you got my letter?"

"I got it."

"Well, what luck did you have? Were you able to reach the Caverhill woman?"

"I reached her—but that's as far as the luck went. I got nowhere with her at all."

"Meaning that she couldn't tell you anything?"

"Wouldn't. It's my own fault, I suppose," Bannister admitted. "When it came right down to it, I wasn't able to think of a good approach. The minute I brought up the name of Wells McGraw, the woman froze on me. She denied knowing him—and kept on denying it, when anyone could have seen it was a lie. For my part, I just couldn't persuade her I hadn't come after blackmail."

"What! Blackmail?" The other quickly scowled. "Ah. I see . . . Yes, I suppose we should have guessed that might be her reaction. Well—too bad. But perhaps we can get to her through her uncle."

"Arch Caverhill's dead. He was shot and killed this morning."

That was a shock; the syndicate man stared at him. "You aren't serious! Just what's been going on here?"

Bannister told him, bringing a look of utter incredulity to the other man's face. Unable to contain himself, Selden finally interrupted him in mid-sentence. "Murder! Are you positive? You could be mistaken. It might only have been a wild shot from those people in the buildings."

"It was murder! I saw Frank Stroud give the signal, and I saw his gunman carry it out. Knowing, of course, doesn't make any difference. A man in my position can hardly bear witness, or testify to it in court; I did go so far as to tell the marshal and at least put the thought in his head— and as a result I almost ended up in a cell, headed for New Mexico and my own hanging! So I've done all I could, and it wasn't much."

"No, no—of course," the syndicate man agreed impatiently, with the wave of a hand. "Whatever way he died, the fact remains that Arch Caverhill was an important man in this state; his death will cause a host of repercussions. And from our point of view it couldn't have come at a worse time."

"But, it's come . . ." Jim Bannister added, "You still haven't said what you're doing here."

"That's true," the other nodded. "Very well— I'll try to be brief. I think you already know about the struggle that's been going on inside the Company, ever since you shot Wells McGraw. I've been leading a fight to end the kind of strong-arm methods that resulted in your wife being killed by a wild bullet, from one of those thugs McGraw hired in the Company's name. I've got the old guard on the defensive. Nobody at Chicago headquarters will admit hiring a creature like McGraw to do the Company's dirty work. I even searched the files, but they've been tampered with—any letters, any scrap of correspondence involving McGraw has been removed, by someone who doesn't dare take the blame."

Bannister said, a shade impatiently, "You've told me all this before."

"Did I tell you I think I've managed to narrow it down to a single man? One of the kingpins—a fellow by the name of Haywood; I've been after that sonofabitch a long time. If we can somehow tie him to McGraw, there's every chance I can knock him off for good."

And climb over his body? Bannister finished silently. In his predicament, he had of course to be thankful for an ally as powerful as this Boyd Selden. Still, there was a sour taste to knowing he meant no more to the syndicate that had outlawed him, than as a pawn in a high-stakes battle for Company control.

He must have shown something of his feelings, for the other man commented dryly, "I must say, you don't appear very enthusiastic. Anything that strengthens my hand in Chicago, has got to be a break for *you*."

Jim Bannister said, from the depths of the bleak mood that had settled on him, "In time, a man begins to wonder if he believes in breaks . . ."

His shrewd gaze studying Bannister, the syndicate man agreed, "It has been a long siege. Is it two years, now, that you've been on the dodge from that murder conviction?"

"A little longer."

"Well, it never pays to lose hope. I was just thinking of someone we both know, who would be very disappointed if you did. Someone, I take it, that you met since you've been outside the law; a young woman I ran into a few months ago in—what was the name of the place? Morgantown? She was considerable help to me," Selden pointed out, "at a time when I was anxious to get in touch with you. I was wondering if you still hear from her."

"Stella Harbord," Bannister confirmed. "Yes, she's been standing solidly by me."

"A fine woman, I thought. What's more, she struck me as one who would be glad to marry you if she had the chance. So, you see," Boyd Selden went on, "though we can't bring back the past, or all that you lost because of the Company—still, with the Company's help, perhaps there can at least be a second chance for you."

It was a subject Bannister had no wish to discuss with this man. He said coldly, "Because of this 'new development' you spoke of, I suppose . . ."

"That's correct; and I'd better explain: It's

the Pinkertons again," Selden told him. "They now have evidence that clearly puts our man in Houston at the proper time, and they're almost certain he had a meeting there with Wells McGraw. Haywood has always denied any such connection, of course. But there's one person who should be able to help us prove, once and for all, that he's lying."

Jim Bannister shook his head. "You mean Emily Caverhill. And I'd say you can forget it! There'll be no help from her, certainly not now— her uncle's death is bound to have hit her hard. I doubt she would even be made to listen."

The other man said, with cool assurance, "I didn't travel this distance, on a matter this important, to give up without an effort. Obviously you made a botch of things. It looks as though I'll just have to go on to Broken Spur and have a try at the woman myself."

Bannister stiffened. "The mood people here are in," he retorted, "you'll be lucky not to get your head blown off. Especially if Wes Niles should get the idea you're another blackmailer!"

"I'm not asking you to come with me, if you've lost your nerve."

For a long moment Jim Bannister could only stare at the syndicate man, trying to control a temper that was frayed by ill fortune and the loss, somewhere along the line, of a night's sleep. "Don't worry about my nerve!" he snapped, finally. "Whatever this business means to you or the Company, *I'm* the one who has the most at stake. Right now you're my only hole card—and I've got to try and protect it!

"So get back in that buggy. If it's physically possible to see the woman, we'll do it together. . . ."

Chapter XIV

When the wagon carrying Arch Caverhill's body down from the Holbrook Lease pulled into the yard at Broken Spur, with its silent escort of riders, only Wes Niles accompanied it on to the house; the rest peeled off and headed for the corrals where they wearily lit down and began to unsaddle. Niles had already caught sight of Ridge Decker, comfortably seated in a rocker on the deep veranda, his boots up on the railing. Now he spotted others who had been with Stroud in the gunfight that morning—a couple lounging yonder in the doorway of the cookshack, another strolling up unhurriedly as the wagon drew to a halt. Something in the way they seemed to be making themselves at home caused the muscles in the foreman's jaw to set dangerously.

The door of the house opened then, and Emily Caverhill came down the steps with Frank Stroud solicitously at her elbow. Niles dismounted, to stand beside his horse while he watched her approach. The pallor of her face showed how the morning's tragic happenings were telling on her. She halted at the wagon and put one hand on the iron rim of a wheel, as though to steady her as she looked wordlessly at the blanket-wrapped shape the box contained. It was Stroud who reached and drew back a corner of the cloth, revealing the lifeless face beneath it.

Emily's cheeks pinched in and her eyes shut tight, and in alarm Niles saw her sway slightly; he wondered if she might be about to faint.

He wasn't the only one to feel concern. Suddenly a big-boned, gray-haired woman was there to shoulder Stroud out of the way and put an arm around Emily Caverhill, while she started handing out instructions in a no-nonsense manner. This was Sybil Ryland, who had been Arch Caverhill's housekeeper since as long as anyone could remember and who had no qualms about issuing orders to the hard-fisted men of Broken Spur.

Now she gave Wes Niles a scolding. "Are you just going to stand there and leave him lie in that old wagonbed? You know better than that! Have one of the boys help tote him up to his room for now, until we can get ahold of the preacher and make proper arrangements for burying him. Now, you move!"

"Yes, ma'am," Niles said meekly, and signaled the puncher on the wagon seat to climb down and lend a hand.

As he moved around to lower the tailgate, Mrs. Ryland quickly turned Emily away. "You just come along with me, honey," she said. "These men can handle everything. Margie!" That fetched her daughter, and she and the blonde girl, between them, succeeded in moving Emily away from there. Niles approved, glad not to have her watch while her uncle's body was slid from the wagon bed and carried, an awkward weight in its blanket wrapping, up the stairs to the room and the bed where he had lain so many nights, through so many years.

With those fierce eyes closed above the predatory beak of a nose, Arch Caverhill looked much gaunter and frailer than he ever had in life. Dismissing the puncher, Wes Niles slipped off the well-worn, expensive boots and set them on the floor beneath the edge of the bed. With hands that trembled a little from grief and anger, then, he drew a quilt up to the dead man's chin. All in good time, Sybil Ryland would take charge of washing and preparing the body for burial; for now, it would have to be enough to hide the blood that had soaked his clothing. Niles stepped back, just as Emily and Frank Stroud entered the bedroom.

For a long moment all three stood silent, looking at Arch Caverhill who might, from the look of him, have only been asleep. A warm wind lifted the curtains at the window, bringing the scent of rangeland and forest and the quiet sounds of the ranch yard below. The men waited for Emily to speak; when she did, it was to ask Wes Niles, in a leaden voice, "Were any of the crew hurt in the fighting?"

"That new hand, Joe Honeycutt. He's got a bullet in him and until it's dug out I don't think he ought to be moved; so I left him up at the Holbrook place, and I've sent for the doc. I'm sure he'll pull through if we take the right care of him."

"I'm counting on you to do whatever has to be done," she said.

Stroud had been scowling during this; now he remarked irritably, "I see no use upsetting her with the details of ranch business, at a time like this!"

Wes Niles felt an angry reply swelling in his throat, but out of respect for Emily he forced it back; it was the woman herself who quickly pointed out, "Frank, I asked him a question. He was only trying to answer."

"All right—so he answered." The cold stare rested on the foreman, an open challenge. "Just now I'm sure there must be plenty of things that need his attention. To put it another way, Niles— has it occurred to you that we might want to be alone?"

Niles met the look, and struggled with a deep animosity that seemed almost beyond his power to bottle up. The man's proprietary attitude where Emily and Broken Spur were concerned— the presence of Ridge Decker downstairs on the veranda, and those others that Stroud had brought here with him: He didn't have to like any of it, even if he was only a hired foreman and this man was the one that Emily Caverhill—so suddenly, now, the new and sole owner of a ranch the size of Broken Spur—had chosen to marry.

Deliberately, he turned his attention from Stroud and told the woman, "I got a message I promised to give you, Emily. It's from Harry Lantry."

She frowned. "Yes?"

"He wanted me to tell you how sorry he is for everything that's happened. And Emily, I believed him—he looked pretty bad shook up. He insisted he hadn't the slightest idea which of his people could have done for Arch. I believed that, too."

She considered for a long moment, her forehead puckered in a frown. Then slowly she nodded, and her breast lifted on a tremulous sigh. "I have to agree. Harry Lantry never seemed the kind of man who'd have wanted that. But, oh! It's all such a waste!"

"Any war is," he said grimly. A moment later he was gone, dragging on his sweated Stetson as he took his stocky shape out into the upper hallway, and down the stairs.

Frank Stroud looked after him with an expression of unconcealed dislike. "The man is a boor!" he declared flatly. "I don't know how your uncle put up with him. All I've been able to get out of him is argument!"

Emily stirred out of her private distress enough to say, in protest, "Oh, no, Frank! Wes Niles is an excellent foreman—none better. And he's been much more than that to me—I count him as a good friend, someone I can always depend on."

She missed the stabbing look he gave her. With a shrug Stroud said, "Well, luckily there's no longer any need to be dependent on him. After all, you haven't forgotten this is Saturday. And tomorrow afternoon—"

"The wedding . . . No, of course I hadn't forgotten. But, is it right? After—this!" She looked once more at the motionless figure on the bed, leaving Frank Stroud thoughtfully regarding her.

"You think we should postpone it?" He spoke carefully. "I understand, naturally—but I don't agree. It's more important now than ever, that we go right ahead as we planned. You can't possibly manage Broken Spur all by yourself," he insisted. "Emily, I want to help you share this burden. It's what Arch would have wanted.

"Just last night—riding up there on the mountain—almost his last words to me, were to say how much he hoped for from this marriage. If anything should happen, he'd be happy knowing you weren't to be left alone."

"I see . . ." Emily had come about again, as he was talking, to meet his gaze with a troubled frown. She started to say something but instead swung away and, like someone in deep thought, moved across the room, nearly to the window; there she faced him, silhouetted against the blast of sunlight. He couldn't help but hear the real distress in her voice when she finally answered.

"Frank, I've done some thinking, these last few hours. It's the hardest decision I've ever made; but I know now that I can't marry you. Unless—"

His face hardened perceptibly. "Unless?" he repeated.

She took a breath. "Unless it's honest and aboveboard, every card dealt square to the table."

"I don't understand! You're thinking that I—?"

"No, no! It's *me!* There are things about me that my uncle and I have made every effort to keep hidden. But I can't live with it any longer—I can't build a marriage on a lie."

For a long moment he studied her anguished face. "I was beginning to wonder," he admitted finally. "Ever since yesterday evening, at the hotel. This stranger—this fellow that called himself Bonner: Would he have anything to do with what you're saying?"

"He has everything to do with it! His coming has made me see I have to tell the truth, before it's too late. Whatever happens then, happens!"

"All right, suppose you tell me. Let's see how the cards look face up."

She stood straight and tall before him, her hands clenched to stop their trembling. But in that moment, before she could speak, a shout

231

lifted thinly through the open window. Something about the sound caused Emily Caverhill to turn and draw the curtain back so she could look down into the yard. As she did, she stiffened.

She did not recognize the single-seated buggy she saw rolling up just now before the house, nor would its leather top let her see who was handling the reins of the animal between the shafts. But she had no trouble recognizing the man named Bonner, riding boldly enough beside the high front wheel. His erect posture in the dun's saddle, the quick turning of his head beneath the Stetson that shadowed his face, the hand resting on his holstered gun—all showed clearly enough he knew the danger he was in.

From under lowered hatbrim, Jim Bannister watched the men of Broken Spur converging on the rented buggy like iron filings drawn to a magnet. The yard had turned ominously quiet, after the first startled shouts of recognition. Now, as Selden halted his rig before the steps of the main house, Bannister shifted position slightly, hipping over to a more comfortable position that brought the gun in his holster into prominence. No one could fail to see the way his hand rested on it, almost negligently.

He was looking for Wes Niles and now he spotted him, just stepping out upon the veranda— Niles had closed the screen behind him and he stood with one hand on the catch, while he stared at Bannister as though doubting his senses. As well he might, Jim Bannister thought sourly. Only Boyd Selden's needling, and Bannister's own determination to see the matter through, could have led him to ride openly into this place a second time.

Another man rose from his chair and moved forward out of the deep shadow of the veranda. It was Frank Stroud's short-coupled gunman, Ridge Decker. So Stroud must be here somewhere, which did not at all surprise him. In fact, he now thought he could pick out, standing somewhat aloof from the Caverhill crewmen, one or two who had been with Stroud in the battle at Holbrook headquarters. Their being here only added one more uncertainty.

Wes Niles spoke, his bull voice carrying in the stillness: "Bonner! Is this some kind of trick?"

Bannister shook his head. "No tricks, Niles," he answered flatly. "I think we've had enough of those, haven't we?"

The other's scowl switched to the one on the buggy seat. "And who's this?"

"Selden is the name—Boyd Selden." The syndicate man answered for himself. He had removed his Homburg and was calmly wiping the sweatband with a handkerchief; now he put the handkerchief back in his pocket, and the hat upon his head. "You're the foreman? And, on receipt of a curt nod: "I have very little time, but there's some business I simply have to take up with Miss Emily Caverhill—much as I hate to intrude, knowing what happened to her uncle . . ."

Wes Niles had lifted his head sharply, his eyes narrowing. "Her uncle! Now, just how would you know about that? Damn it, the news ain't hardly had time to get beyond this ranch. By God, it sounds awful funny to me!"

"Let me assure you—" Boyd Selden started to say; he was interrupted as Emily Caverhill stepped out onto the veranda.

Frank Stroud was right behind her but he halted inside the screen. Bannister saw a questioning look pass between him and Ridge Decker, saw the gunman shrug to proclaim his ignorance.

Emily came as far as the steps, and as the sun struck her face Bannister saw at once she was under some great strain; somehow he wondered if it was entirely the result of her uncle's death. Her own look was fastened on Bannister. "Wes!" she demanded of her foreman. "What's he doing here?"

But then Boyd Selden was out of the buggy and approaching the steps, hat in hand. "Miss Caverhill?" he said. "I must apologize for this, but it's a matter of great importance. May I give you my business card?"

She dragged her eyes away from Bannister long enough to glance at the card as it was handed up to her. He wasn't sure she even saw the printed words, or heard Niles' hurried explanation: "The man insists on seeing you, Emily. He won't tell me why."

" 'Western Development Corporation'," she read aloud, slowly, and frowned in perplexity. "If this is some business concern of my uncle's, I—I just don't know." Her voice faltered. "It's too soon. I'll have to talk with his lawyers and with Mr. Niles, before I could possibly—"

"If you'll just let me explain, privately," the syndicate man said. "This hasn't to do with your uncle. The matter is—well, I would say it's personal."

"Personal?" Bannister saw her expression change and harden; he had time to think. That was probably the wrong word to use! The vagueness had left her. Her look swung to Bannister and she said, in a tone of bitterness, "Would it be the same 'personal' business *you* wanted with me, last evening?"

Before he could speak, Selden answered for him. "Yes, Miss Caverhill. As a matter of fact, we are together in this."

"I see." And Bannister could all but hear the thought behind her words: Another blackmailer! There was almost a kind of satisfaction in knowing that Boyd Selden, for all his cocksure confidence, was managing this no better than he had done, himself.

But then the woman's expression underwent a subtle change. Though her voice remained ice-cold, what she said next took Bannister completely by surprise: "Very well, Mr. Selden—and your friend, too. Will you both come inside, please? There's something I want you to hear. You too, Wes," she added. Bannister saw the foreman's look of puzzlement and, he thought, of sudden alarm; but as she turned back into the house Niles merely nodded and opened the screen for her, afterward waiting, with unconcealed hostility, for Bannister and Selden.

Having no idea what might be coming, Bannister dismounted and tied the dun to a railing of the veranda. Selden had already snapped on the buggy weight, anchoring his rent horse; the two of them went up the steps and inside with Wes Niles silently following. Emily Caverhill was waiting in front of the unlit fireplace in the living room—in almost the very spot where Margie Ryland had stood yesterday for the unsuccessful masquerade Wes Niles had put her through.

Frank Stroud was there as well, leaning against the massive center table with folded arms and a wary expression on his face. There were no formalities, no suggestion for anyone to take a seat; the woman looked for a moment from one to another, then at last drew a breath and spoke, in a voice that was vibrant with resolution.

"You couldn't have come at a more suitable

time, Mr. Selden. I'd like you to meet Mr. Stroud—the man I'm engaged to marry. When you arrived, I was just about to tell him something I felt he had a right to hear. Now you can hear it too—you can all hear it—and after that there'll be no secrets for anyone to bother about."

Wes Niles' head jerked up. There was horror in his face. "Emily! No!"

She refused to look at him. Instead she turned to Frank Stroud who was staring at her in fierce puzzlement, and who now demanded, "I want to know what these two men could have to do with you, or me. I've certainly been waiting long enough to find out!"

"They're here," she answered, her voice level, "with information they obviously thought my uncle would pay to keep the world from hearing."

Stroud put his cold stare on Bannister and Selden, in turn, and it was freighted with the utmost contempt. "So! I begin to understand. And what was this—information?"

Niles, with a defeated shake of the head, raised both hands and let them drop. Emily Caverhill met her fiance's question without flinching. "You mean, you haven't guessed? What did you think I was doing, in Denver—a woman alone, without money or any way to support myself. . . ."

Bannister saw the man's face turn to iron. "You almost make it sound as if you'd been on the streets!"

"But that's it, Frank. That's my secret! These men knew; they've had the Pinkerton Agency finding out for them. They even traced me all the way back to Houston; I'm sure they have every detail fully documented! I could try to make excuses," she went on, her voice almost without expression, "if there was any point. But one thing I've decided: I will not pay blackmail! Oh, there was a time I'd have given anything, to save my uncle from learning the truth—but as it turned out he'd known all along, and didn't even care!

"And now I've told the man I thought I was going to marry; so at least I'll be able to face my conscience. And as for you," she finished, looking at Bannister and at Selden with withering scorn, "you've only wasted your time, after all. Because now, you see, it doesn't matter any longer *who* knows about me!"

Into a heavy silence, Boyd Selden spoke. "Miss Caverhill," he said, with more real feeling than Bannister had thought him capable of, "this is all very unfortunate! You must believe me— no one had any thought of blackmail. It wasn't even you we were interested in, but a man named Wells McGraw. We learned from the Pinkertons that you'd known him in Houston; there was just a chance you could tell us something useful concerning him, if we could persuade you. And we had to try—in a very real sense, it was a matter of life or death!"

Emily Caverhill was staring at the syndicate man, and she looked stunned; her cheeks were, if anything, even paler than before. "Is this the truth?" she asked finally.

"It's the truth, Miss Caverhill," Jim Bannister answered her. "I wanted to explain last night, but I wasn't able. I'm terribly sorry."

"And you're telling me," she said dully, "that I've made a confession for nothing!" She turned an anguished look to Wes Niles. "And the effort you and Uncle Arch made to keep my secret— I've thrown all that away. . . ."

The foreman said quickly, "What was done, was only to spare your feelings, Emily. You mustn't think, even for a minute, that Arch Caverhill was—*ashamed* of you!"

She allowed herself the faintest of smiles. "But of course I know that!" She drew a breath. "Well," she said then, "it's done, and I can't say I'm sorry. It was a burden I couldn't have carried any longer—not into a marriage!"

Bannister was watching Frank Stroud. It was interesting to try reading Stroud's face, in the wake of Emily Caverhill's revelation. He saw a medley of expressions there—surprise, and a flash of cold anger; but then, visibly, these emotions were erased and gave way to a compassion that, to Bannister's eyes, looked completely phony. Stroud pushed away from the table where he had been leaning; he went to the woman and placed both hands upon her shoulders, turning her to face him. He said, "I'm glad you told me. I won't say I enjoyed hearing it—but there's no reason this has to make any difference."

Her eyes studied his face, as though in disbelief. "You mean—?"

"As far as I'm concerned," he told her flatly, "nothing has changed. After all, what's been said here in this room doesn't need to go any farther."

"And—you still want to marry me?"

The slightest of shrugs. "Everything's arranged; it would look damned odd to back out now. I'm willing to go through with it."

Bannister had suddenly had all he could take, "And why shouldn't you be?" he said, in a tone that brought every eye to him. "You've worked hard enough to get your hands on Broken Spur. You've even done murder for it!"

Chapter XV

He thought someone gasped. Stroud's head came around; his stare pinned Bannister. "Would you like to say that again?"

"I think you heard me." He looked at the foreman. "I don't know if you're aware, Niles, but I was on the hill above the Holbrook place this morning. I watched the fight with Lantry. I saw your boss ride over to that draw to have a talk with Stroud—and then he rode out into the open again, and that's when he was shot."

Wes Niles wagged his head impatiently. "It's no secret you were up there. It wouldn't surprise me if you saw Arch killed."

"That isn't all I saw! I can tell you the name of the man who killed him, and it wasn't any of Lantry's people. It was Stroud's gunman—Ridge Decker."

Frank Stroud snapped, "Nonsense!"

"Fact!" Bannister continued, not even looking at him. "Stroud gave the sign; Decker used the rifle. It was deliberate—one shot was all he needed."

Livid with indignation, Stroud turned to the woman. "*You* don't credit any of this?" But as he saw her stricken face, and the way she drew back as though from the touch of his voice, his own expression changed. "By God, I could almost think you do!"

"Frank!" she began. "I—" And then she faltered and her lips visibly trembled.

"If he knew such a thing," the man insisted, beginning to show the first faint hint of desperation, "why is this the first he's said about it? Why isn't the law here to arrest me?"

Bannister had a partial answer for him. "I've talked to Marshal Blackman, but you know very well he can't arrest anyone outside the town limits. And it's my understanding the sheriff's office is seventy miles from here."

"You've got that right," a new voice said. "But it don't matter to *you*, mister—that's one place you'll never live to see!"

It was Ridge Decker who stood in the archway, with a gun in his hand and leveled at Jim Bannister; a person might have wondered how he managed to move so quietly, as to open the screen and come in on them without anyone hearing a sound. Now, Bannister looked into those curious muddy eyes and what he saw started a coldness working in him. He was very careful in that moment not to let his hands make any move at all.

Frank Stroud was the first to react. Stroud was furious—he had intelligence enough to see in this the wreckage of his own credibility. He took two strides forward, his face darkening with rage as he cried, "What the hell do you think you're doing? Put that gun away. That's an order!"

He got no more than the barest of glances. "I've just quit taking orders from you," Decker told him. "Nobody pays me enough to hold still and be nailed with a murder rap!"

"But, you fool! Don't you see he was only making talk? There's nothing he can do!"

"Absolutely—I intend to make sure of it!" And he turned again to Bannister, showing his teeth with the feisty belligerence of a small man toward a larger one whom he recognizes as his superior. "You and me, big fellow," he said. "We're leaving here." He crooked a finger of the hand that didn't have the gun. "Just walk toward me . . . walk easy!"

Jim Bannister merely looked at him; making no move to obey—determined that, whatever else, he would not show fear in front of someone like Decker. But now Boyd Selden, who had been hearing all this with a look of shocked disbelief, found his voice and exclaimed in protest, "What do you intend to do with this man?"

The gunman looked at him. "That would be between us."

"You'd take him out and put a bullet in him? Because he named you for a murderer? All you'd do is prove he was right—and remember, there are people here in this room who can bear witness!"

The muddy eyes narrowed a little, studying him. "You know, you've got a point? But there's a way to take care of it . . ."

Wes Niles must have thought he saw a chance, then.

Obviously Niles was no kind of gunman; nevertheless, he still wore the belt holster he had taken up to the Holbrook Lease with him—and this was the man who had killed Arch Caverhill and would even dare threaten Emily herself. That may have given him the impulse that led the Broken Spur foreman, not normally a reckless man, to make his try while Decker's attention was centered somewhere else.

But Decker must have owned remarkable peripheral vision, for he caught the movement out of some corner of his eye and he whipped about, searching for it. For one fatal instant, Niles' weapon caught in the holster; frantically he jerked it free, but then it was already too late. The other man fired. Niles, hit, staggered and fell against one of the room's heavy armchairs; it toppled with him but kept him from going all the way to the floor. The revolver dropped from his fingers.

Even so, he had bought a brief moment for Jim Bannister. Reflexes that had been honed fine, through months of living with constant danger, worked now almost automatically; yet Ridge Decker was almost too fast for him. The little gunman hadn't even waited to see Niles go down. He was already turning back to confront the man he considered his enemy, the smoking pistol swiveling. Bannister had his own weapon clear by then. The two exploded nearly at once. Somewhere beyond Bannister's elbow, a window went out with a smash. It was Ridge Decker who, with a look almost of disbelief, crumpled and started to the floor, twisting as he dropped.

The crash of gunsound was numbing to the ears. Blinded by the smear of muzzle flash, Bannister stood for a moment confused and vaguely aware as someone went by him, boots pounding the bare planks of the flooring; an elbow jostled him in passing and nearly threw him off balance. He shook his head to clear it, then, and saw Wes Niles clinging to the chair where he lay half-sprawled, blood already showing on the sleeve of his right arm that dangled in a way to suggest Decker's bullet had broken it. Emily Caverhill stood as though frozen with shock.

Boyd Selden said, into the echoes of the guns, "Your man Stroud is getting away from you!"

Bannister nodded. He pointed at Wes Niles. "See what you can do for him. And the woman." After that he turned and ran from the room, as the man he was pursuing let the screen door slam behind him.

When he broke out upon the veranda, Frank Stroud had already reached the dun horse

Bannister had left tied at the foot of the steps. He made a move to grab the anchoring reins, but the animal didn't like him and it acted up, dancing away at the end of the leathers. Its manner apparently changed the man's mind: Stroud left the horse and ran on into the yard, and Bannister leaped down the steps in pursuit.

He was suddenly aware that the outbreak of shooting had brought men hurrying up from every quarter of the yard. Stroud saw a couple of his own crew among the rest and he raised a shout, calling on them by name: "Fetters! Workmen! Quick—bring up the horses!"

Then, as Bannister paused at the rear of Selden's rent buggy, Stroud halted and turned, and the six-shooter Bannister had always suspected he wore under his coat was in his hand. He was firing as he brought it up. His bullet whanged off the metal rim of the buggy's wheel and the startled horse lunged forward a couple of uneasy steps, taking the rig with it. Bannister was left exposed. Not hesitating, he set himself and returned the fire, and missed.

At that moment one of Stroud's men, running toward Bannister, tried a shot in midstride but succeeded only in kicking up dirt from the hardpack. Bannister refused to be shaken off his target. He looked through streaking powder-smoke and found Frank Stroud, in the act of bringing his pistol down from its upward recoil;

Bannister caught him in the sights, and touched the trigger. The gun bucked against his wrist. Struck squarely, Stroud was thrown backward and down into the dirt.

The man looked dead enough, but Bannister had to be sure. He approached warily and was forced to swallow back a sudden sickness that rose into his throat, when he saw what his bullet had done. But his own danger wasn't over yet. Shaking off his revulsion, he quickly raised his head.

Those four men of Stroud's seemed to have frozen in the act of converging on Bannister. He stood at bay, measuring them with a quick, sweeping glance as he threw his challenge: "You want to go ahead with this? You realize your paychecks have just stopped. Is it worth taking the risk for nothing, just to find out how many of you I might drop before you can kill me?"

He got his effect. With men who hired out their guns, personal vengeance for the death of whoever had been paying their wages was not generally part of the code. Even so, a man had his self-esteem and it had to be reckoned with. For a moment, in the stillness following the gunplay, the situation hung fire.

Then, somehow, Wes Niles had made it outside to the porch and, braced against a roof support, he held a gun awkwardly in his left hand while the other dangled, bloody and broken. In a voice that was sharp with pain he cried, "Broken Spur! Don't stand there—grab these men and take their guns! Decker and Stroud were the ones who murdered Arch. If these others want trouble, I don't think anyone will care a damn how much you give them. . . ."

The Stroud men heard. They looked at one another, and they gauged the numbers of Caverhill riders who began to move on them in response to the order from their foreman. These four had no one to give an order; discreetly, as with one accord they began to empty their hands. Seeing that, Bannister let go of the breath that had been trapped in his lungs.

On the veranda, Wes Niles seemed to let go all at once. His legs lost their stiffness and he slid slowly down the roof prop, leaving a streak of red across the white paint.

Arch Caverhill being dead, and Broken Spur's foreman for the moment incapacitated, no one of the crew seemed ready to take hold. Jim Bannister assumed command almost without thinking.

The last thing this ranch needed was a pair of corpses; he dragooned the Stroud men to help dispose of them. They showed no particular resentment as he ordered them to fetch up the horses and lash Stroud and Decker belly-down across their own saddles—this was, to them, all part of a familiar game where violence was the normal ending, with no great importance attached to which side won or lost.

Bannister stood and watched them ride unhurriedly out of the yard leading the grimly laden horses, knowing they would quickly get rid of the bodies—it hardly mattered where. Within twenty-four hours, he'd wager they would have gathered such belongings as they possessed and, traveling light, would already be scattered out of this country looking for the next gun job, somewhere else.

Just now, he was more interested in finding out how it was with Wes Niles.

The foreman hadn't yet been moved from where the starch had run out of him and dumped him. He sat propped against the veranda railing while the gray-haired housekeeper, with help from one of the punchers, tended to setting and bandaging and splinting his wounded arm. Emily Caverhill knelt close by, doing what she could but more than likely getting in the way.

Watching her with Niles, it seemed to Bannister she showed considerable concern for a man who was, after all, merely one of her uncle's crew. The Ryland woman apparently noticed it, too. As she finished adjusting a sling for the wounded arm, the housekeeper assured her, "Now, stop fretting! He'll mend just fine. You can have the doctor check it, if you want, but a clean break like this is nothing I can't handle."

"I know, I know," Emily Caverhill said distractedly. "I'm sure you're right. I just can't help being concerned."

"Wes Niles is pretty tough," Jim Bannister reminded her. "I don't think a little thing like a broken arm is going to lay him out for long."

From the way she looked up at him and at Boyd Selden, silently watching, she might almost have forgotten them both. Her frown became guarded, unreadable; then, abruptly, she was getting to her feet and brushing off her skirt. Her hand rested for a moment on Wes Niles' shoulder. When she turned to leave, the hurt man raised his head and looked after her with an expression that seemed to Bannister almost one of open adoration.

At the door, she turned to Bannister and Selden. "Come with me, please," she said.

As they followed her into the house, Sybil Ryland was gathering up the materials which she had used on the injured arm; she put a glance on Wes Niles' frowning face and then in the direction of the door. She said, "If you were to ask me, somebody has suddenly found out who it is she really cares about."

Niles whipped his head around, and angry color flooded his cheeks. "Don't make fun of me!"

"Who's making fun? I've known for a long time how you felt about Emily Caverhill."

"Since the day she first set foot on this ranch

three years ago!" He shook his head as he added gruffly, "But, hell! Who am *I?*"

"A better man," Sybil Ryland told him firmly, "than the one she thought she wanted to marry. Or—was it the man she thought her *uncle* wanted?" When Wes Niles only continued to stare at the toes of his dusty boots, she looked as though she might be losing her temper. "Can't you see you're the best thing that could happen to her, *or* to Broken Spur? If you want that girl, you'll take my advice and go after her! You just might be in for a surprise. . . ."

In the front hallway, Bannister and Boyd Selden had been left standing while Emily Caverhill, with no further word of explanation, went up the stairs alone. As the moments ticked by Selden threw the taller man an impatient look; Bannister could answer it only with a shrug. "I have no more idea than you have," he said into the stillness, "why she called us in here. But she must have thought it was important . . ."

She was back, then, coming down the steps toward them, and she had an envelope in her hand. Even in the shadow of the hall she showed the many shocks she had taken in these last hours; still, when she spoke to Jim Bannister she seemed able to hold herself under firm control. "I'm obligated to you," she said. "Being able to repay you is out of the question; but do you

251

suppose this might be of any help?" She offered him the envelope. "One of the last times I saw Wells McGraw, down in Houston, he gave me this and asked me to keep it for him—he said it could be very valuable to him one day. So, I put it away among my things and somehow never thought about it again—I wouldn't even have remembered I had it, until you came asking questions. Anyway, here it is."

Instead of taking it, Bannister motioned for her to give the envelope to Selden. The syndicate man thanked her with a nod and, as Bannister watched his face, opened the envelope and glanced quickly over the single sheet of paper he took from it. Nothing in his expression would have indicated what he held. He tapped the paper against a thumbnail a couple of times, considering. Finally he lifted his eyes, to ask the woman, "May I keep this?"

"Certainly, if you can use it."

"I can use it." He added, "I can also give you my assurance that, whatever comes of it, you won't need to be brought any further into this, in any way. I promise I won't be bothering you again."

She nodded soberly. "Thank you."

As abruptly as that, their business here appeared to be finished. Selden apparently wanted to go; and Bannister, thinking of the marshal left locked in his own jail, was more than ready to be quit of this country. Staying for Arch Caverhill's burying was, of course, out of the question. A last word for his niece, and a handshake with Wes Niles as they passed him on the veranda; then it was down the steps to the yard, where a Broken Spur hand was busy scattering loose dirt over the dark spot that told where Frank Stroud had bled out his life. As Selden was about to climb into his rent buggy, Bannister's curiosity finally overcame him.

"Well?" he demanded.

The other's deliberate manner was maddening. "What?" Then, as if only just remembering the envelope he had slipped into his pocket: "Oh—I guess you mean this." He allowed himself the meagerest of smiles, as he brought it out again. "It's better than I could have hoped for, Bannister—a letter to Wells McGraw, on Company stationery, in George Haywood's own writing and over his signature! He confirms the hiring of McGraw, and says he expects results that will impress his colleagues, as well as showing the rest of the world that Western Development has no likelihood of going soft. If anyone has the temerity to offer resistance, the letter gives McGraw a free hand in making an example or two—and Haywood isn't much concerned how he does it, if he gets results!

"It's no wonder he wanted to keep ahold of this letter! The time might come when he would need it to protect himself—or perhaps he saw himself using it to lay pressure, some day, on the man who was stupid enough to put such things on paper. But as far as I'm concerned," Boyd Selden continued, "I can go back to Chicago with this evidence and see Haywood's head on the block. What's more, I'm positive I can use it to get you a new trial—perhaps even an outright pardon from the Governor in Santa Fe. At the very least— with the Company's influence and our lawyers behind you instead of trying to have you sent to the gallows—there isn't a doubt in my mind that, in a new trial, your murder conviction can be set aside. As I see it, Bannister, your battle is all but won!

"Man, do you hear what I'm telling you?"

Jim Bannister could not have answered. Standing there in the sun, with the reins in his hands and the buildings of Broken Spur about him and the mountain's head towering to the summer sky, he was overwhelmed suddenly by understanding. It all seemed to come crushing upon him—the many months of running and hiding, the hopes and despair, the times when freedom had hung by a thread, and every man's hand had been lifted against him. To think of an end being suddenly and actually in sight, was almost more than he knew how to handle.

He heard the syndicate man saying, "It looks to me, Bannister, as if all you have to do now is find some safe place where you and that Stella

Harbord girl can keep out of sight and out of trouble, for a short while yet. Once I set the machinery in motion, it shouldn't take me long to get the job done in Chicago, and have a word with that governor. Before you know, you'll be your own man again, with this whole ordeal behind you. How is that going to feel?"

Bannister moved his shoulders, like a man shedding a burden. "It's going to feel damned good!" he admitted; and because he didn't trust himself to say anything more he turned to shove his boot into stirrup, and lift himself into the saddle.

But it was as though the air that filled his lungs had, already, the clean, sweet taste of freedom.

Books are
produced in the
United States
using U.S.-based
materials

Books are printed
using a revolutionary
new process called
THINKtech™ that
lowers energy usage
by 70% and increases
overall quality

Books are
durable and
flexible
because of
Smyth-sewing

Paper is
sourced using
environmentally
responsible
foresting methods
and the
paper is acid-free

Center Point Large Print
600 Brooks Road / PO Box 1
Thorndike, ME 04986-0001 USA

(207) 568-3717

US & Canada:
1 800 929-9108
www.centerpointlargeprint.com